The patterns on Foundry Editions' covers have been designed to capture the visual heritage of the Mediterranean. This one is inspired by the grillwork and balconies of Paris and was created by Hélène Marchal.

CÉCILE TLILI co-founded an alternative school for neuro-atypical children. *Just a Little Dinner*, 2023 winner of the Gisèle Halimi Prize, is her first novel.

KATHERINE GREGOR is a translator from Italian and French. She was also an EFL teacher, theatrical agent, press agent, and theatre director. She created and wrote *The Italianist* blog for eurolitnetwork.com. As a writer, she is the author of published articles and is currently working on her first non-fiction book.

Cet ouvrage a bénéficié du soutien du Programme d'aide à la publication de l'Institut français

# JUST A LITTLE DINNER

CÉCILE TLILI

# Just a Little Dinner

Translation by Katherine Gregor

**FOUNDRY EDITIONS**

# 1

Claudia leans against the kitchen wall. The heat stored in the plaster throughout the day spreads into her hips, back, and shoulders. Her head, ever so heavy, droops forward. Glimpsing the red streaks across her chest, Claudia sinks deeper into the wall, heedless of the marks she leaves on the white paint, her hands still oily from greasing the chicken.

The kitchen is stifling. It's almost eight o'clock, but the sun is still seeping through the gaps in the shutters, roasting her skin. Or perhaps it's the curry that's turned this room into an oven. What was she thinking, making a hot, spicy dish in this weather? Étienne had said a salad would do.

He comes up to her. "They'll be here soon, Claudia. Go and have a shower."

He's cool and clean. He puts a hand on her neck and feels her artery throbbing under his thumb. "Is it making dinner that's got you into this state?" he asks in disbelief. "Go and have a shower, it'll do you good."

Étienne slides his hand to the back of her neck and squeezes it gently, subtly pushing her towards the corridor and the bathroom. It's a slender neck. The chicken's neck has been thrown in the bin, along with the giblets. The butcher insists on giving her all the animal's parts and, perplexed, she always takes a moment to stare at these intruders among that flesh with its orangey skin: the dark, glistening entrails, the bend in the neck, the now harmless spurs.

"Yes, I'm going."

In the bathroom mirror, Claudia's naked body is a patchwork of scarlet and white. She spent nearly three hours preparing this meal. She sliced the onions finely and their persistent smell clings to her hands, refusing to let go of its prey. She diced the carrots and courgettes, soaked the raisins in water, let the oil sizzle in scalding pans. Whenever she could get away from the steam of the casserole for a few minutes, she paced up and down the flat, looking for a cushion to plump up, a knick-knack to reposition. The table is as pretty as a doll's dinner set. She has placed bowls of pistachios and olives all around the living room.

Claudia turns the shower mixer tap to *cold* in the hope that the jet of chilled water may wash off not only her sweat, which smells of curry and garlic, but these hideous red blotches too. She watches the water running between her breasts, over her belly, already a little filled out, then down her legs into the plughole. Staring at the twists and turns of her veins under the translucent skin of her feet, she feels a vague sense of shame bubble up inside her. She wanted to play the perfect hostess at her first real meeting with these friends of Étienne's. She threw herself into the role wholeheartedly. The staging had to be perfect and the meal delicious, and now it's time for her to spruce herself up. That's what Étienne really expects, of course: "Go and have a shower, it'll do you good" meant "Make yourself presentable, dress up, match the decor."

She rubs herself with the towel so hard she chafes her skin. The redness that vanished from her cheeks after the cool shower returns with a vengeance as she thinks about the imminent encounter. Claudia slips on a black dress and applies make-up, trying to conceal the dark red blotches that keep spreading over her face. She wonders if she should wash again; she thinks she can detect a lingering smell of curry under the scent of lemon verbena left by the soap. But it's too late: her guests will be here soon.

Claudia looks at herself in the bathroom mirror and sees herself the way Étienne's friends will: a bland, awkward woman with nothing to say, a woman he picked because she's undoubtedly good at taking care of their home, and because there's no chance she'll overshadow him. She has painstakingly and foolishly devoted all her energy to becoming this caricature – the opposite of how she would have liked to come across – and to appearing the contrary of what they are: always busy, snowed under with work, unable to find five minutes to address practical issues because they're sucked into the whirlwind of business and Paris life.

She should have thought about what to say to them and how to present herself. She could have constructed her character instead of throwing herself body and soul into creating the decor.

Self-effacing Claudia. She's heard this epithet so often and wishes she could apply it literally. Efface herself, disappear. Not contend with inquisitive or indifferent looks, spare herself the embarrassment of noticing the shadow of boredom in people's eyes as soon as she utters a few words. Of course, she can always keep quiet: keep quiet, smile, laugh at other people's jokes. But she knows they'll only judge her even more cruelly: Claudia, the trophy girlfriend, the woman of no interest.

She joins Étienne on the sofa. He's leafing through documents he brought home from work. Without looking up, he pulls Claudia towards him, his hand large enough to grab half her ribcage. He drums his fingers on and between her ribs. Black, white, black, white. His fingers pick up the tune of Claudia's panic-stricken heart. She wonders if she should ask him about Johar and Rémi, about what they do besides their jobs, what they enjoy. There may still be time to get ready for this encounter. But Étienne wouldn't understand, he would look up, puzzled, from the contracts he's reading and tell her to ask them herself.

Unable to sit still, Claudia gets up and goes back into the kitchen. In the living room mirror, beneath a wreath of plaster fruit and vines, the young woman in the black dress who glances at her through her dark locks has a ball of fire where her face should be.

2

Johar walks in the twilight. She asked her driver to drop her off a few blocks away from Étienne's building. She needs some air before getting cooped up for the evening. She walks slowly, in no rush to arrive at this dinner party she wasn't expecting and is already finding annoying. She takes her time to inhale the heavy scent of this summer evening. The avenues here are wide. There are windows with striped awnings swaying gently in the breeze. The rustling of the trees accompanies her footsteps and their canopy forms a protective arch above her head.

Here she is already on Boulevard Raspail, outside Étienne's building. She sits on a bench and takes a deep breath. A few swathes of grey have appeared in the sky. Gusts of wind toy with the dry leaves, warm blasts of air hitting her in the face. A thunderstorm is badly needed to break this late-August mugginess at last and wash away the day's sweat and weariness. She throws her head back and looks up. Above her, the foliage of the plane trees forms geometrical ochre shapes against the blue backdrop of the sky, reminding her of the stereograms from when she was a teenager. She tells herself, like she did back then, that if she stares at the abstract patterns long enough, she might see the 3D image they conceal.

She wishes she could spend the evening on this bench, watching the city play out its story before her. She never sees the city any more. She leaves the granite and concrete monster where she works for the cool saloon car that takes her back to her large flat in Paris's western *banlieue*. She gets home, has a shower, joins Rémi sometimes, but mostly finds herself alone because, tired of waiting, he's gone out or else is already asleep.

She never walks at night any more. There is no night in the business district that has become her life's stage. There are no smells, no footsteps slowing down. The greyness is so dense, it masks the light of summer evenings. A few puny trees, their roots trapped in hideous stone vices, try to escape notice, as though ashamed to disrupt the uniformity of this mineral citadel. Johar doesn't see them any more. She walks on the flagstones, head down, pounding the ground in her square-heeled shoes – if they were too narrow they would get trapped between the granite slabs and she might break her ankle. Like all the women over there, she goes around in a dark suit, her hair smoothed. She never lifts her eyes to the top of the steel and glass towers. She rushes from one appointment to the next, her earphones glued to her ears.

Johar's thick buttocks form a comfortable cushion on the bench. She put on weight during the holidays. Too many sweets. She tells herself that if the hellish pace of her working days has one silver lining, it's that it staves off the temptation of sweets. She wishes she could raise her legs and press her knees against her chest, in the teenage posture she thought she had forgotten. But her suit is too tight. It's the only suit she managed to squeeze into this morning, an outfit that's far too warm for this time of year but which seemed more appropriate for lunch with Carl, her CEO, than a dress bursting with her summer curves.

She must go on a diet. She actually started one today without intending to: she was so nervous at lunch that she couldn't eat a thing. Now she's hungry and feeling too hot. Tiredness is crushing her on this Boulevard Raspail bench. Johar thinks she'll never be able to stand up. She knows she has a thousand things to do: hurry to this dinner party – her lateness already borders on rude – consider the decision Carl has asked her to make, and call him to give him her answer. Instead, she lets all these thoughts slide away and basks in the comforting drowsiness spreading over her.

Johar takes her time. She stalls. Leaning against the back of the bench, she feels the hot, sticky air flowing around her. She moves her hand slightly, as though to burst the storm-bloated sac that surrounds her. She listens to the sound of footsteps on the pavement, plays at guessing who the quick, cheerful gait belongs to, and slowly turns to face the reality of the passer-by she has invented. She pictures herself morphed into an owl, staring at humans, rocked by the wind in the trees.

Around her, Boulevard Raspail rustles with calm, polite life. Couples dressed as though on their way to Mass slip out of the buildings lining the street. Johar fantasises that if she listens carefully, she will hear the drone of the conversation that must have started without her in Étienne's flat. It probably involves art, culture, travel, and smug smiles. On the taxi ride, she resented Rémi for making her come to this dinner party, but then, after all, she thinks, it's thanks to this invitation that she can enjoy these stolen moments – almost certainly her last for a long time. Her last before the big leap.

If only she could be forgotten on this bench.

So she can make the most of these instants that hang from the branch of a plane tree. So she can scan the quivering city with her owl eyes.

Her phone vibrates. It's Rémi. It's a quarter past nine. *"Don't worry,"* Johar taps in response to her husband. *"I'm on my way."*

# 3

Claudia hears heels clicking in the stairwell. She presses on the knot forming in her stomach.

Rémi arrived a long time ago, but, after a few initial civilities, she managed to take refuge in the comforting solitude of the kitchen. Naturally, he noticed her flushed cheeks, made fun of her flushed cheeks, acting embarrassed that he'd interrupted her and Étienne in the middle of a quarrel – or perhaps in the throes of passion, she's not sure, it was all too witty or too crude for her, but she didn't ask him to repeat, she laughed and felt the blotches on her face turn the colour of a cockerel's crest.

There's actually nothing else for her to do in the kitchen. Dinner is ready. Through the glass wall between the kitchen and the living room, Claudia sees the two men, indifferent to her absence. She slips behind the counter that divides the room in half, relieved to be out of sight. She retreats a few more steps until her back is against the familiar warmth of the wall next to the window. The large black and white chessboard-patterned tiling stretches from her feet to the glass wall. A defenceless queen, she has already lost the game.

She tries to let herself be lulled by the melody of the two men's voices and forget about Johar's impending arrival, forget that she'll soon be flushed out. She can make out Étienne's voice in particular, shriller and more nasal. Rémi contributes only brief, enthusiastic exclamations. He's yapping, she thinks. Claudia listens to their tongues clicking against their palates between sips of the whisky brought by Rémi. If only she, too, were allowed to dissolve some of her anxiety in alcohol.

Before she huddled back in her burrow, while she was serving the men their drinks, Étienne grabbed her by the wrist with a subtly possessive gesture, turning his irresistible face, a mixture of sharp edges and smooth curves, towards her, giving her his brilliant society smile. She wondered if he was laughing at her angst, increasingly palpable as Johar's arrival grew nearer, or if he was trying to conceal his embarrassment at her awkwardness.

All Claudia recalls of her previous and only encounter with Johar is her loud, gravelly laughter, which revealed a wide gap between her two front teeth. The remainder of the evening is buried in her memory under a padded veil, although she doesn't know whether her brain threw it there in retrospect in order to hide a painful wound generated by the events, or if her headache really did make everything feel and appear blurry.

It was at the beginning of her relationship with Étienne, just over two years ago. Before he decided to let her wall herself up in her shyness, when he still seemed smitten enough, or at least proud enough of his conquest, to want her to meet his friends. With the same persistence he'd once used to persuade her, his young physiotherapist, to have a drink with him, then to spend the whole evening with him, and, much later, to move into his flat, he'd now talked her into going to a friend's birthday party in a Paris bar. All day, Claudia tried to persuade herself that it would be easier for her to go unnoticed in a large gathering, hoping she'd find a dark corner where she could wait inconspicuously for the hours to go by. Étienne picked her up from his place after work and they were among the last guests to arrive. She saw at a glance that her plan to hide was futile. No bench to slip away to, only four high tables already swamped. Everywhere, small groups, forehead to forehead, champagne glass to champagne glass, speaking loudly to drown out the music, catching waiters by the elbow as they circulated with trays filled with golden treats.

More eager, when it came down to it, to have fun with his friends than to show off with Claudia, Étienne literally hurled her into Johar's arms before joining a group that welcomed him with excited chirping. By way of introduction, he just shouted to the two women, trying to talk over the din, "Claudia, this is Johar, Rémi's wife – I've told you about her, you're going to love each other, Johar is the most brilliant, genuine woman I know."

*And nothing to say about me,* Claudia thought.

Johar grabbed Claudia by the shoulder and in this spontaneous hug and the directness of her slightly gap-toothed smile, there was an almost maternal warmth that Claudia wanted to wrap herself in at first.

"Claudia, Claudia," Johar cried, "at last a face to the name I've heard so many times! I was beginning to think Étienne was hiding you, and now I understand why: he's found a treasure!" Then she burst into a spectacular laugh.

And, with naïve trust, Claudia listened to this flattery, believing it had a note of sincerity. With the same weakness as when she thought she saw love and perhaps even admiration in Étienne's eyes, and the same vanity as when she assumed he had chosen her because he perceived the nugget buried under layers of shyness and self-effacement, she thought that Johar would be able to understand her. For a moment, she imagined opening up to Johar.

Then a man came up to them and whispered a few words into Johar's ear and she exclaimed, "What? What?" looking as though she was taking Claudia aside at first, and Claudia, unsure whether Johar was asking because she hadn't heard or because she was surprised, smiled like an idiot, and the roar of the music suddenly became unbearable, and Johar turned her face entirely towards the man and let go of Claudia's shoulder. Claudia's throat tightened with a feeling of abandonment so ridiculous it still makes her blush now.

Alone, severed from the anchor she had briefly believed she'd found in Johar, Claudia started drifting, dejectedly, through the sea of partygoers, shunted about between nervous waiters and guests whose brilliant smiles were never directed at her. Claudia felt by now that these strangers were giving her embarrassed looks. *I'm the only one on my own*, she thought, stupidly trying to adopt a pose, pretending to glance at her phone, and the shock of abandonment gave way to anger and a feeling of humiliation thumping fiercely in her head. Étienne was not looking at her, of course, Étienne, who had cajoled her into inflicting this torture on herself. As for Rémi, whom she had already met a few times before, he simply gave her a nod and a smile, and didn't even take the trouble to come and say hello. Everyone around her was flowing about, making and unmaking small groups, clinking glasses, as though they were performing a choreography and only Claudia did not know the steps. She could see Johar's body in particular – even though it was much bulkier than hers – flow with ease, as though her round curves and thick helmet of dark hair shielded her from impact. Moreover, Claudia regularly heard her belly laugh, but didn't dare look at her for fear she would realise that, since their brief exchange, Claudia had found no one to talk to, and feel sorry for her.

She'd promised herself not to be taken in again and had stood up to Étienne with a determination he hadn't seen in her, by declining every invitation after that. He could go out as often as he pleased, but without her. And he certainly hadn't held back.

She had tried to put up the same fight when, a few days earlier, Étienne announced that he had invited Rémi and

Johar for dinner. He had never asked anyone over since he'd been living with Claudia, and she assumed it was a non-negotiable premise: she took care of the flat and of him, with a smile, as long as he did not place her in danger inside her fortress. Especially not by letting Johar in. Johar, whom he considered brilliant and genuine, Johar, who was too clever to take an interest in her, Johar, who was everything she was not.

But this time Étienne did not give in. Much to her surprise, he even raised his voice to make his point. This was his home, after all, and he didn't leave her any options, it was an important dinner, a business dinner at which grown-up subjects had to be discussed – subjects he didn't bother revealing to Claudia but whose total priority she was supposed to grasp. And no, it couldn't be anywhere else, Johar had no time to entertain (*unlike me, who has nothing else to do*, Claudia had inferred) and lately no longer accepted invitations to go out. You had to ask her to your home to be sure she'd turn up.

Claudia could only comply and try to dissolve her anxiety in a curry sauce.

# 4

Johar is assaulted by the smell as soon as she steps into the flat. The voice of Ella Fitzgerald, greeting her in its throaty tone, and the soft lighting in the connecting rooms seem to affirm that she has just walked into an elegant, understated bubble. And yet the powerful scent of curry contradicts that.

While Étienne hugs her with unexpected affection, Johar remembers her first Paris flat, in Rue Cail, around the corner from the Gare du Nord. The walls were so thin she could hear the neighbours whenever they rowed, fortunately in unfamiliar languages most of the time, every step in the street echoed in her ear, and every washing machine cycle in the adjoining flats would make her head feel like it was rolling in sand, like a wave. There was a smell of curry everywhere, in the corridors of the building, outside every restaurant. She ended up not having people round and started surreptitiously sniffing the crook of her arm before arriving at the office to make sure the smell hadn't stuck to her skin. Since her days in Rue Cail she's kept off spicy foods, and even demands that her mother make two different sauces on the rare occasions she still has a meal at her parents' – one following her age-old recipe, the other bland, especially for her daughter.

Johar glances at the impeccably laid table in the dining room and heads to the living room. Rémi waves at her from the sofa. She wonders if it's the soft cushions or the alcohol fumes that prevent him from standing up to greet her.

"Claudia," Étienne calls out, "come and say hello to Johar." Johar wants to laugh at the way he addresses his girlfriend, as though she were a child, but restrains herself when she sees Claudia come up to her, stony-faced. Her every feature seems tired, there are red streaks over her cheeks and throat, and her eyes are elusive behind her severe locks of hair.

"Hello, Claudia, how are you?" she asks, trying to reconcile what she sees with what she remembers of their previous encounter: a tall, exquisitely understated brunette who'd made her think Étienne's taste in women was growing more refined, Étienne, who had up till then collected blonde trainee lawyers still rosy with adolescence.

"Fine, thank you – and you?" Claudia replies like a polite little girl.

"Long day. I've had a hard day. I'm tired. Sorry I'm late. I warned Rémi it was a bit hit-and-miss to get together for a dinner party after the summer holidays, when it's always very busy, but he said I could get away with being a tiny bit rude among friends. So here I am, late and empty-handed... But I'm glad we can spend some time together – you two still have that beautiful summer glow – this way we can extend the holidays together a bit."

Then to put Claudia at ease – she hasn't budged, her tall, stiff frame is still rooted at Johar's side – she adds, "It smells delicious! I've not had anything to eat all day. What have you cooked for us?"

"Claudia insisted on making chicken curry, it's her speciality," Étienne replies on her behalf. "Shall I get you a whisky?"

Not waiting for an answer, he heads to the kitchen and brings back a glass half-filled with ice cubes.

"Sit down, Johar, make yourself comfortable." Unconcerned with Claudia, who is standing awkwardly between the armchairs, Étienne sits back down next to Rémi and pours Johar much more than she can reasonably drink. He takes up all the space with his long, slender limbs, in ruthless contrast with Rémi, who is slouching, his chest over his belly, the bottom button on his shirt about to pop.

"We should thank Étienne for inviting us," Rémi says to her sarcastically, "so we can actually spend some time together."

"You know perfectly well I do my best... but you're right. This dinner party's a brilliant idea, Étienne – here we are, the three of us, like in the good old days, and I'm delighted to get to know Claudia better. Claudia, won't you come and sit with us? Sorry, Étienne, for usurping your role as host, but your partner might as well make herself comfortable."

As Claudia complies and sinks obediently into an armchair opposite her, Johar darts Rémi a look of annoyance. She wonders what she's doing here and misses the peace and quiet of her bench. She doesn't feel up to an entire evening of Étienne's sickly-sweet politeness, Claudia's unease, and Rémi's grumpiness towards her – he begged her to come, and now he's got the cheek to try and settle scores with her in public.

She takes a gulp of whisky, too quickly. She's used to all the demands of a director's life, except skipping lunch. As soon as she misses a meal, her head starts spinning dreadfully, like the ice cube at the bottom of the glass she's fiddling with while silently looking at her hosts and her husband.

Étienne starts fussing over her. He read the feature on her in *Challenges* magazine last month: "Johar Léger, the tough cookie of tech." He even seems to have learned it by heart, since he's enthusiastically reciting long passages from it. He has remembered the message drilled into the journalists by her PR department, she'll be able to tell them they've done a good job: her major achievement as COO isn't just having revolutionised the company, but also having revolutionised the country by winning and expertly implementing a number of contracts to digitalise some jewels of French industry, as well as – the ultimate achievement – several government ministries. Étienne has retained a few soundbites in particular, which he enjoys repeating, like "her iron fist" and "a woman who moves mountains", and she mellows in spite of herself. Étienne channels all the allure of his Hollywood-star face into his flattery act, his grey eyes boring into hers, his full, sensual lips revealing his impeccably white teeth as though they represent all the gifts he has in store for her. He's always been terribly good at this.

And yet she hated that article. First, the title: *Johar Léger*... The surname never fails to strike her as odd when attached to her first name. She has often regretted adopting Rémi's surname when they got married, just to make things easier, to avoid always having to spell her surname whenever she introduced herself. In addition to this regret there's now the irony she can't help hearing in the adjective léger, light – which she used to scoff at when she was younger because it didn't go with Rémi's roundness – when she looks at the pictures in the magazine and sees the marks of time in her chubby cheeks and unattractive double chin. Finally, she detests the same old anecdotes that have been told to death, the anonymous comments from those who leap at the chance to settle scores, and the ones from so-called friends who can only flatter her in public.

At the thought that she'll have to endure another wave of these veiled publicity pieces with her forthcoming appointment, Johar takes another sip of whisky. A muffled tune starts throbbing in her skull.

Étienne pauses his praise for a moment, apparently searching for words.

"Since you orbit so close to the sun, you must be privy to the secrets of the gods. Are your lot really going to buy Neria? Is the younger sister going to devour the elder?" Then, very softly, as though apologising for asking, he says, "No doubt you will personally have a say in the choice of legal advisers for this deal?"

Johar raises her glass of whisky a little higher. Through its frosted surface, Étienne's long arms stretch in every direction and multiply, he's like a spider clinging to the sofa.

So that's what all this was about. A professional favour. Between old friends, as Rémi said, there's no need to stand on ceremony. He could have just called her. She would have appreciated a phone call much more than having a whole evening ruined. She can't wait to tell Rémi exactly what she thinks, since he is no doubt an accomplice to this charade.

Yes, she does have a say in choosing the legal advisers, and a lot more besides. Étienne will have to play an encore of his scene of boundless admiration after he finds out which position she'll soon be occupying in the new organisation. As for keeping Étienne on rather than hiring others, she doesn't really mind. But it's a bit too early to answer. This evening, Johar feels like playing.

She acts as though she hasn't heard his last question, puts her glass down briskly, and goes up to the fireplace in the living room. She picks up a red ceramic fruit, runs her fingers along the edges that break up the smoothness of the sphere like the seams of a rugby ball, and admires the tiny crown on the flattened top. Then, turning to Claudia, who hasn't said another word since the initial pleasantries, exclaims with slightly forced enthusiasm, the whisky already producing its effect, "I guess I have you to congratulate for all the feminine touches, Claudia. These pomegranates are gorgeous!"

# 5

*Pomegranates.* Silence, followed by an aftershock that propels her heart deep into her chest.

She's been dreading this moment ever since Étienne and Johar started talking. Since Johar blew into the living room like a whirlwind, since she ordered her to sit in the armchair, since she took over the room with her loud voice and her laughter, Claudia has found herself in a scene she's experienced a thousand times before. Lost on a chair at the back of the classroom, she quakes at the prospect of being quizzed by the teacher. Banished to the end of the family table, she stares intently at her plate, hoping her mother won't ask her *what's new* in her life. Sitting with Étienne's friends, she prays they won't notice that she doesn't understand a word of their conversation. This evening, she's tried her best to catch snippets of it, but she knows nothing about Johar's work, nothing about these people Étienne mentions as though she were familiar with them.

And lightning has finally struck her, as always.

"These pomegranates are gorgeous! Where did you unearth these little treasures, Claudia?"

All of a sudden, they're not talking about digital transformation any more but about decoration. Before she has time to open her mouth, Étienne comes to her rescue.

"I brought them back from Iran. You know, there are images of pomegranates all over the Middle East. Even beyond the Middle East, in fact: they're mentioned in Greek mythology and even in the Bible..."

Claudia watches her partner, who doesn't even glance her way as he joins Johar by the fireplace to show her his ceramics. Feeling a blend of anger and distress bubbling up inside her, she wonders if she'll ever be able to solve this contradiction: she wants to be invisible, but resents them all deeply for making her so.

The pomegranates aren't hers, obviously. Nothing carries her mark here. When she moved in with Étienne two years ago, she arrived with three suitcases he accommodated in his cupboards. She had sold the furniture in her studio online. As for ornaments, she had given a few away and thrown away many. The odd one or two had secretly found their way back to the childhood bedroom her parents had, to her surprise, kept in their flat just as it had always been. Everything she owned had suddenly seemed poor-quality and tacky. She had decided not to bring the fragments of her previous life to Étienne's flat. Rather, she wanted to discover the world she had only guessed at in the days when he'd fought so militantly and persistently to win her over. He would cut his working days short so he could wait for her outside her practice, then whisk her away on a whirlwind journey, though they were still sitting at a table in a Paris bistro. Étienne's warm, caressing voice would transport her through space and time, painting the panoramas of distant lands, immersing her in the colours and scents of civilisations unfamiliar to her. Whenever he placed his hand on hers, he would crack her shell. To Claudia, who was stifling in a cramped life, Étienne threw open the door to a new world, as broad and beautiful as him.

Her gaze drifts from the pomegranates to the glossy spines of the art volumes on the bookcase, then gets lost in the thickness of the Persian rug. She clings to these things as to so many memories of her first moments with Étienne. With the tip of her foot she follows the arabesques woven in the wool and notices that her ankle is trembling slightly.

She tells herself that she just needs a little longer. She'll find her niche. There's no doubt about it. There isn't the shadow of a doubt, because he wants to have a child with her.

Étienne turns to her, his slender fingers stroking the varnished surface of the fruit. "Claudia, won't you put your courgettes in the oven? Johar's starving and, frankly, so are Rémi and I. Do you think we could sit down to eat in fifteen minutes? That'd be perfect."

# 6

Étienne won't stop talking about pottery. Johar was hoping that her interest in the pomegranates would create a diversion, but he has gleefully grabbed this opportunity to describe his tastes, his travels, and his encounters. As usual, Étienne talks about himself. He briefly goes into the dining room, but before Johar can enjoy a minute of peace, he returns, carrying a vase with a delicate blue pattern.

"Here, look. Hold it. Does it remind you of anything?"

"No. I don't know. Did it use to be on this mantelpiece?"

"No, no – I mean the pattern. Surely you recognise it?"

Johar mechanically runs her fingers over the vase, following the geometrical outline of the turquoise stars. Étienne can't contain himself any longer. "Nabeul. It's pottery from Nabeul."

Nabeul. Images of the small Tunisian coastal town sweep over Johar. Nabeul, which, like a termite queen, laid a constant flow of ceramics, its entrails producing monstrous quantities of dishes, plates, and bowls decorated with blue and green rosettes, threatening to drown the hordes of tourists who thronged the narrow streets, their arms scorched by the sun. Johar recalls how, as a child, she worried that those countless pairs of legs, red and brown, would trample the precious crockery that poured out onto the pavements.

She responds mechanically to the self-satisfied smile lighting up the face of her friend whose erudition had once fascinated her, so much so that it had played a crucial role in defining the middle-class, intellectual ideal she was striving towards. She wonders what Étienne expects from her by talking about Tunisia. *Maybe he thinks I'll give him the contract,* Johar says to herself with irritation, *because he contributed to the GDP of my parents' country of birth by spending a few dinars on this vase.*

"I don't think I've ever set foot in Nabeul," Johar says, lying. "It's like a temple of cheap craft down there. Actually, it's not like you to have gone on holiday there."

"I stopped there on my way to the Carthaginian city of Kerkouane. Did you know it's the only city that stayed Phoenician? All the others, Carthage in particular, were Romanised later, but Kerkouane is still as it was when it was abandoned, centuries before the common era."

Rémi speaks from the depths of the sofa, where his friends have forgotten him. "No point in rubbing salt in the wound, Étienne, we don't know Nabeul, we don't know Tunis, or Djerba, or anywhere else. You know holidays in Tunisia are banned in our family."

Johar interrupts him sharply. "We've had this conversation hundreds of times. It's too built-up now. They've totally ruined the coastline."

"But there are still some forgotten gems," Étienne continues. "In Kerkouane – on my own, because no one's heard of the place– I walked through the ruins overlooking the sea, among dry stones and olive trees, as the sun was setting; it was beautiful."

Johar turns away, uncomfortable about being propelled into Étienne's intimate memories. She doesn't think she has ever seen Tunisia at the time of day he describes, when everything is veiled in gentle pink. She feels as though she has only ever known her parents' country oppressed by the light and heat. Her Tunisia is about waking up, clammy, on foam mattresses thrown on the floor in her aunt's small flat. The ruthless bite of the sun when, after following her cousins down the stairs of the building, she'd find herself hurled onto the waste ground that acted as a square in front of the small housing estate outside Tunis. The ball games in sticky dust, running down the shadeless city streets whenever an adult gave them a few coins to go and cool down in the Magasin Général with over-sugared fizzy drinks.

Johar thinks with bitterness about how her parents traded the outskirts of Tunis for the same narrow walls, the same stairwells with chipped paint, and the same grey housing estate esplanades in Noisy. They left behind their parents, the graves of their ancestors, and their reassuringly gravelly mother tongue to spend their early mornings in the Noisy bakery, kneading bread that would never be truly French.

Of course, they did all that for her and her brother. To give them the right to succeed. The duty to succeed. Johar has followed their instructions to the letter. She worked, patiently, she fought, and she has risen, higher and higher.

Johar takes a few steps back into the living room to escape from Étienne's volubility. She looks at Claudia, behind the glass wall to the kitchen, arranging orange flowers with bulging bellies on a serving dish. Their delicate ruffs sag with the weight of the stuffing and remind Johar of an image she had forgotten. She recalls an impromptu swim in Cape Bon, one evening after a long day in the car. She remembers running through hundreds of wildflowers opening on the carpet of sand, cool at last. Her mind travels back to those frail little flowers, modestly bowing their heads; she hears the blend of joy and fear of the children lost in the calm, black expanse of the sea. She feels the roughness of the towel her mother used to dry her with after her salt bath, and the softness of her arms.

Her mother has tried calling her several times today. She should ring her back. But she must phone Carl first. "Étienne, if you don't mind, I'm going for a cigarette on the balcony before we start eating."

# 7

A shadow drifts behind the glass wall into the kitchen and sinks onto the stool opposite the one where Claudia has taken refuge.

"Are you all right, Claudia?" Rémi asks. "What you've cooked smells nice."

"Thanks... The courgette flowers will be ready soon."

She immediately wants to bite the inside of her cheeks. She hates her servility, the docility with which she slips into her mistress of the house act.

Rémi makes himself comfortable. He puts his glass of whisky and the bowl of olives he has brought from the living room in front of him. He smiles at her, his elbow on the counter, head resting in his hand. He seems to want to talk to her, unlike Étienne, who, as soon as Johar slipped away to the French windows for a smoke, announced he'd grab the opportunity to send a few urgent work messages.

Of all Étienne's friends, Rémi is the one Claudia has

seen most of, and is certainly the one she finds the least intimidating. She feels guilty because she realises that her relative trust in him comes from his somewhat unattractive appearance, the shoulders that slouch over his torso as though trying to conceal its almost feminine curves, and his cheeks, which look like two little goatskins storing the excess flesh on his face. Rémi gives off a kind of reassuring simplicity Claudia vaguely attributes to his job – he teaches Economics to a lycée class that prepares students for elite universities, so she assumes he must be used to addressing individuals who are younger and less learned than him and that his role is to give them confidence. That and maybe his relatively modest family background.

Even for a few minutes, Rémi is glad to escape the living room, where the atmosphere is still strained. He has always liked kitchens: the smell of heated oil, the fringe conversations, the secrets told around the stove. He takes his time to observe Claudia's face, an elusive face, but with a gentleness that makes you want to tame it. He listens to her breathe the way a child listens to the heartbeat of a sparrow in his hand. He takes pleasure in this fragility, so far removed from Johar's overwhelming self-assurance. Something about Claudia reminds him of Manon, and he wonders if he'll find a moment to call Manon this evening. He is aware of the fact that, since the summer, he's felt the need to speak to her every day, that he doesn't sleep well at night if he hasn't heard the husky tone of her voice at least once that day, and that the restlessness in his hands ceases only when they skim the curves highlighted by the freckles studding Manon's back.

"Is your work at the practice going well?" Rémi asks to start a conversation.

"Yes," Claudia replies.

She knows she must continue, bounce back, but she doesn't know what to say. It comes so easily, so naturally, to them and to others, to talk of everything and nothing.

Claudia bullies herself into responding. "My patients are well. I mean, unwell enough to give me work, but they're well. Generally better, afterwards." Her shambolic delivery seems to echo between the kitchen walls for a long time. Rémi laughs. *He thinks I'm being witty*, she thinks.

"And the business side is going well?"

"So-so. It's not always easy. Because most appointments are now booked online, my diary is getting more and more unpredictable, so I can have days when two thirds of my patients cancel. But the regular bills still have to be paid..."

It's easy for her to pick up the leitmotif about the hard life of self-employed professionals, endlessly heard in her family circle. From her father, a psychiatrist, and her mother, a gynaecologist, the talk was never of care or patients, but of schedules, fees, and investments. Her parents jointly ran a business entirely aimed at the production of material comfort for themselves and their six children. While her father, a shrewd financier, maximised the accumulation of wealth, her mother, logistics coordinator-in-chief, planned her long consulting days, her offspring's multiple extracurricular activities, and the holidays on the Île de Ré with equal efficiency. A team of young au pairs, the armed wings of the maternal war machine, would take them to school and music theory classes, and, in the summer, to windsurfing lessons. They would butter the bread in the morning and read stories in the evening. In her parents' Taylorist view of education, there was no room for moments of shared dreams or comforting cuddles. Children's talk was rationed at home, permitted only at weekend lunches. *My one-to-one conversation time with Rémi has already exceeded what I had with my father*, Claudia thinks. Deep down, she is absolutely certain that her parents never knew and still don't know their children. They simply arrange them in two groups, the easy ones and the difficult ones, and from the way her mother squints whenever they meet, Claudia knows she belongs to the second category.

Rémi prompts her again. "How did you come to choose physio?"

*By chance and by myself*, Claudia thinks. *By default and luck.* When, at the start of her final school year, she asked her mother for some "personal advice", the latter shook her head. "It's not for me to prescribe you the pill, Claudia," she said. "I'll refer you to a female colleague." It was therefore at one of the regular Sunday lunches that Claudia, her face red with emotion, had to share her wish to follow in her parents' medical footsteps, despite her average school grades. She recalls the two perplexed slits on her mother's face, her father's taut smile as he muttered a few words to himself about the difficulty of self-regulation and self-esteem in teenagers, and the blank faces of her siblings, focused on taking the floor themselves when their turn came to speak. The chicken gravy in the boat was trembling in time with the knocking of her leg under the table. A few weeks later, she enrolled on the physio course.

"I wanted to care for people," Claudia replies, giddy from opening up like this. "I like healing, and I do it better with my hands than with words." She's not sure about telling him more, about the surprising poetry of bodies lying on her physio couch, the skin, sometimes smooth, sometimes gritty like semolina, the protruding shoulder blades, the beauty spots like coffee grains. To pluck up the courage, she pictures herself straightening the curvature of Rémi's spine, massaging the Christmas tree-like folds in his back. She could tell him about the surprising strength in her hands, which squeeze, stretch, and twist. But he's not listening to her any more. Claudia turns to see where Rémi's gaze has wandered. On the living room balcony, Johar is tapping nervously on her phone.

"Who's she texting like that?" Rémi says with a huff. "Funny how, practically overnight, we've nothing more to say to each other. We don't understand anything any more – that's if we ever did."

He picks up his glass of whisky, abandons the last olives drowning in their brine, and leaves Claudia without a word.

# 8

Resting her elbows on the wrought-iron rail, Johar takes a drag of her cigarette and enjoys its pungent burn. The sky has taken on an electrical colour, as though the aerials bristling on the slate rooftops in front of her have brutally discharged all the day's tension. Her foot on the planter, she narrowly avoids knocking over the glass she has wedged between two sprigs of lavender. She tells herself her lungs are worth charring for the freedom this unshakeable alibi gives her to escape at any moment. Cigarettes may be the only link between the teenager she used to be and the woman she has become. The only visible scratch in the varnish she has spread over her life.

As soon as she finishes her cigarette she'll ring Carl. Or, to be precise, as soon as she finishes her cigarette she'll take another sip of whisky, then she'll ring Carl. She promised to give him an answer by 9 p.m. He is going to point out that she's late. And yet he was the one who insisted she take the time to think it over. "So you can talk it over it with your husband," he said, although she's not sure if the irony in his words was intentional. In any case, the deadline was no more than a formality. You don't turn down a position like that, which, more than a logical next step, is a feather in her cap. What he's giving her is true validation.

Johar thinks about her odd sense of alienation at lunchtime. All around her, the floor for the Oryx executive board was vibrating with excitement because of the secret, and the buzz of delight that had crackled on the line through the many phone meetings held during the holidays turned into a roar as soon as the team were gathered again at the skyscraper in La Défense. Carl walked into her office across the large open-plan area, his ochre shoes sliding on the carpet. There was a hint of a smile on his face, but the sun bouncing off his glasses prevented Johar from reading the expression in his eyes. He suggested lunch. Walking beside him towards the brasserie crushed by the monstrous mass of skyscrapers, out of breath and sweating, Johar realised how ridiculously she was walking in order to try and keep up with her boss, and how grotesquely her heavy breasts were bobbing under her blouse. The flood of heat through the Grande Arche, like a flow of lava, seemed to distend shapes and dilate time.

She tried to regain her composure when they started having lunch, as they continued their conversation about the current hot topic in a serious whisper. When the tone grew more solemn, when, like a conspirator, Carl summarised what would be at stake in the forthcoming merger (she already knew it all by heart – a hundred thousand workers worldwide, a turnover of more than ten billion, and securing double-digit growth) and asked her to take the reins of the whole enterprise, with him as non-executive chairman, Johar forced herself back into her shell, that of a woman bundled up in her suit which was too tight and too warm. But she felt incapable of fully inhabiting her body as an unusual feeling of being somewhere else swept over her. She nodded and replied mechanically, vaguely concerned that her boss, who was no doubt expecting signs of joy or pride on her face, would instead find an inscrutable mask. Red juice was oozing from the steak on Johar's plate. She hadn't touched it. She promised Carl she would give him an answer by 9 p.m.

Johar takes a drag from her cigarette. She realises with a hint of bitterness that this unfamiliar sense of being disconnected from herself has deprived her of the intensity of a moment she has pictured a thousand times, a victory she's hoped for a thousand times. Is she unprepared? Perhaps it's the effect of summer. Her skin is still steeped in a holiday scent, and there are still a few grains of sand stuck under her fingernails. Lovely holidays. Especially the last few days, when she and Rémi had the large house to themselves, after their friends and the friends' children had gone. She would get up early in the morning. He would sleep until late. She drank her coffee while staring deep into the Mediterranean down below. She would listen to the song of cicadas growing louder as the sun rose. In her nightdress, she would walk down the path lined with fig trees which led to the cove with its clear water, and would take her first swim in the sea. Cruise ships drifted in the distance, while Johar got drunk on the immense blue of the sea.

Johar watches her cigarette burn down between her fingers the way you watch the last grains of sand trickle down an hourglass, the way you see their progress speed up as they rush down the narrow neck. She lets her gaze sweep over the blueish hills formed by the zinc rooftops opposite her and enjoys the shrieks of the children in the street enjoying their freedom during these final days of August.

The city smells of dried grass and dust. The cigarette end has turned cold between her index and middle fingers. Étienne's overpriced whisky tastes like the cheap whisky she used to mix with Coke at the engineering school parties, a long time ago, when she was young. Johar takes her phone out of her pocket. There's a green strip flashing on the lock screen. Maman. It always startles her to see the word Maman. Despite all the distance Johar has put between herself and her mother, there's still this word, so intimate.

Her mother has tried to reach her again, but hasn't left a message. Johar pictures her face behind the phone screen as last time she saw it, back in January: her grey hair, worn too long, gathered in a hasty plait; the corners of her eyes and mouth drooping as though weighed down by a feeling of disappointment that grows stronger by the day. Over the years, the fury of curls around her face has calmed down – grey hair is probably softer than dark hair, Johar thinks. Perhaps she is now more comfortable with her frizzy hair, or perhaps she just couldn't care less about anything any more – for one reason or another she seems to have forsaken the small pastel-coloured scarf Johar had seen her wear since childhood. Johar thinks about the time she spends fighting with her own mane, the hours by the mirror armed with a hairdryer, the contortions to reach the back of her head, the smell of burnt hair that inevitably goes in tandem with achieving this beautiful, thick, smooth mass. She imagines herself for a moment at the next shareholders' AGM, with her jumble of curls hidden under a pastel-coloured scarf.

She drafts Carl a long message that includes pride, warm gratitude, and her wish to take up the future organisation's many challenges. She deletes it. She writes *"I'm in"*, then deletes that.

Through the corner of her eye, she sees Rémi approach the French windows, his face expressionless. He gestures at her that it's time for dinner.

*To: Carl*

*"Give me a little longer. I'm sorry. I'll let you know in two hours max."*

Johar presses *send*.

# 9

Claudia watches Étienne and his guests through the glass kitchen wall; they are now beyond the living room, gathered around the dining room table. Their conversation is drowned out by the roar of the extractor hood she has just switched on. Étienne does not want her to open the window for fear that the smell of curry will bother the neighbours. The setting sun has left dense surges of heat in its wake. Claudia opens the oven and a scorching blast of air immediately hits her in her face. She wipes the beads of sweat above her lips with the back of her hand. She takes out the platter and puts it on the worktop.

The three friends are facing her, in a tableau framed by the steel fittings of the glass wall. Johar and Rémi are sitting side by side. Standing behind them, Étienne is getting them to try the burgundy he brought up from the cellar this evening. He has turned on the ceiling lights, and in their golden glimmer Rémi swirls the first sip, blood red, in his glass, a smile of happy anticipation on his face. Étienne strokes the label on the bottle.

Bent over the worktop, Claudia transfers the courgette flowers onto the plates, taking care not to tear them because they are filled with stuffing. She hurries, afraid her meal will get cold. Étienne give her a sidelong glance from the dining room. Claudia feels a dull ache in her belly. She wishes she could sit down for a minute and wait for the spasm to ease. She wishes someone would put a comforting hand on her shoulder and chase away her anxiety, which, she thinks, is now being voiced by her body.

Étienne comes in. The moment he steps into the kitchen, the smiling mask on his face suddenly drops. Claudia feels the cramp in the hollow of her belly grow stronger. She feels a vague wish to cry, not sure whether it's because of the pain, the fear, or the shame. She does not dare complain to Étienne. And yet she wishes he would look after her. Just for a moment. Will he take better care of her after she's given him the news?

*Give him the news.* Hope and fear join hands and squeeze Claudia's heart. They have not relented their grip since her appointment with Doctor Edelman three days ago.

Claudia stopped using birth control in late June. It was a decision taken with Étienne, a decision as filled with light as the beginning of summer. The two of them were going to spend two weeks in the Luberon. They were going to make a baby. They were going to explore this vast area of life that was unknown to them – parenthood – and perhaps discover a new complicity there. But then the holidays gradually took on the drab colour of semi-dried lavender. During the ten days he spent with her, Étienne, as usual, patted her hair mechanically while reading or listening to music; perhaps he made love to her a little more often; then he had to get back to Paris early to try and get in on a deal, and left her on her own in the large house in Ménerbes.

While Claudia was on the pill, she did not have periods; she was glad it saved her from that degrading side of womanhood. But, since June, her period had refused to come. Something was out of sync. There was always something dysfunctional in her. She did not dare mention it to Étienne. In secret, she made an appointment with Doctor Edelman for the last Monday in August. No sooner had she walked through the door of her gynaecologist's consulting room and Audrey Edelman looked at her with her gentle eyes, than Claudia felt two fat tears trace ridiculous lines down her cheeks. Audrey was as golden as a butter croissant, her long blonde hair almost white from the sun, her shoulders given a pretty shape by her linen sweater. She was the kind of woman Claudia would normally have found scary, with her overwhelming femininity and sensuality, and yet as soon as she came close to her, Claudia felt waves of gentleness that made her melt. She wished her mother were a gynaecologist like Doctor Edelman. And, sometimes, she wished Audrey Edelman were her mother. Doctor Edelman examined her in silence, except for her deep humming, which she seemed unaware of, then half-smiled at her. "You're not getting your period because you're pregnant, Claudia. Congratulations!" Then, to dispel the shadow she had probably noticed on Claudia's face, she added gently, "It's good news... isn't it?"

Claudia's first thought was for her mother, who would consider her mind-bogglingly stupid if she heard. Her second thought was for Étienne – how would she explain to him that she had seen her doctor without telling him in advance? Fresh tears appeared and rushed into the furrows created by their predecessors. Doctor Edelman asked no more questions. She continued her examination, explained how to do the follow-up for the pregnancy. At the end of the appointment, she gave Claudia a small card on which she had written her mobile phone number. "You can call me. If you ever need to, or just if you feel like it."

Étienne is growing impatient. "Everything's ready, Claudia. Can I take the plates?"

"Just a minute, let me add a few herbs and it'll be done."

Étienne drums nervously on the worktop with his hands. Deep down, he's seething because he's bending over backwards for Johar, Johar who presumes to arrive three quarters of an hour late and then sulks at everyone. He's got his best bottle out of the cellar. He let poor Claudia spend the afternoon cooking. He's tried to angle the conversation towards their mutual interests, but clearly culture and art – actually, not even art, but *crafts* – are pleasures too sophisticated for Johar. And yet Étienne cannot afford to drop either his false smiles or his smooth voice tonight because he really, really needs this contract.

He wonders how he could have let things at the office slide like that. First it was a few barely noticeable slips. Two loyal clients leaving him, one for a competitor and the other one, even worse, for one of his colleagues. A partners' meeting he wasn't invited to. One of his closest colleagues, almost a friend, leaving the boss's office one morning, avoiding his eye. Étienne can't manage to reconstruct the logical sequence of this series of events and whether he lost his clients because he lost his mojo, or the other way around. But the figures no longer leave any room for doubt. He is having a disastrous year and it will continue to be so unless he brings business in, and straight away. He has put his survival on the line this evening.

Étienne looks at the granite worktop where Claudia is putting the last bit of garnish on the plates, at the counter, at the perfectly minimalist kitchen furniture. His gaze wanders to the large mirrors in the dining and living rooms, which respond with their images ad infinitum, to the century-old parquet he enjoys hearing creak under his feet. He could never give all this up. On the contrary, he is programmed always to have more; always bigger, always more beautiful. He shuts his eyes and thinks of the dreadful irony that a backward step, a demotion, would mean at the very moment he has decided to *get ahead* in life, as they say.

Next to him, Claudia lays sprigs of coriander on the plates, focusing on her task. He looks at her long, narrow nose, her high cheekbones, her tight lips. Face-on, she always seems a little hazy, but her profile is more defined and harder. He chose this woman out of defiance, to prove to himself that his charm could have an effect even through the miasma of shyness that practically stifled her, and, above all, because he knew that his superiority over her would never be put in doubt. Tonight, he feels queasy at the thought that she might one day feel sorry for him.

"It's ready, go for it."

Étienne takes two plates and heads to the dining room, with Claudia right behind him. Johar will not leave this flat until she has promised him the contract.

## 10

Johar looks up from her phone. Étienne and Claudia arrive, a plate in each hand, in a ridiculous procession. She wonders why this woman feels she needs to hide behind her partner and why he needs to take credit for dishes *she* clearly spent hours cooking. On her left, Rémi is enjoying small sips of the burgundy. She hears revolting sounds of suction, as if he's giving the rim of his glass sloppy kisses.

At this moment she hates them all. To be honest, it's herself she hates above all. How could she have written that to Carl? *"Give me a little longer. I'm sorry."* She never acts sorry about anything. She never shows hesitation. She's stupidly let herself be troubled by her mother's phone calls, and her mother has really not picked a good day to touch base with her daughter. She's been thrown by Rémi's insistence, by this sour tone he never usually adopts with her. She has put the job of a lifetime in jeopardy just so courgette flowers wouldn't get cold.

The company's senior management: it's been the secret dream in Johar's mind for years. To other people – her friends, colleagues, and the press – she will express her joy at being able to choose the direction in which she will steer this one-hundred-thousand-strong ship, her pride at leading the clients of Oryx and Neria to new technological horizons. The words are already formed and lined up in her throat, ready to unleash their terrible platitudes as soon as she opens her mouth. But the truth is that this promotion will have the sulphurous scent of revenge.

Johar remembers the total absence of shame in the eyes of her first clients when, once they'd got over their astonishment at her first name being a woman's and not a man's, they would size her up, trying to assess through her coffee-toned complexion, her hair – too stiff to be natural – and sometimes through the depth of her cleavage, the extent of her competence. The extent of her competence in software and how capable she was of drawing the last drop of sweat from the developers she supervised. Year after year, she managed to hold her own against their prying looks and seal, one by one, all the cracks they may have been tempted to explore – the faint trace of accent inherited from her mother, the occasional language infelicities she let slip when she first started out. She managed to stand out in the company through her hard work, her tenacity, and her pugnaciousness, even. Johar thinks about the nights she spent correcting contracts, rewriting lines of code, her stomach in knots preparing meetings with furious clients or employees that needed dismissing, and finds herself craving the look of submission in her colleagues' eyes. She pictures them, all those men – always older, always whiter, always maler than her – lined up in their impeccable suits, with their good manners, their depressingly linear CVs, and she dreams of the triumph of the immigrants' daughter over all those whose careers were written from birth.

*"Give me a little longer. I'm sorry."*

Did she get frightened? Did she, Johar, the warrior, the fighter, let herself be overwhelmed with anxiety, like a child? Perhaps, like everybody else, she's ended up being afraid she wouldn't get there, that she's not good enough. Unless, on the contrary, she fears the position isn't worth all she has sacrificed for it.

And yet she hates this idea of sacrifice. She didn't sacrifice anything; she chose. She chose this path, arid and solitary, that has gradually distanced her from her friends, her parents, Rémi; a path where the silence is in no danger of being disturbed by a crying child. It now appears before her like a bridge suspended over the void, where the slightest sidestep could push her into the abyss of the unknown.

Johar turns her phone face down to escape its mesmerising light. She takes slow breaths to calm down. She can hear children shrieking through the window. She glances at her watch – almost 10 p.m. – and wonders what they're doing in the street so late, then remembers it's still the summer holidays. She tries to make out their words, but all she grasps is shrill, joyous babble. She takes a sip of wine and resists the temptation to get up from her chair and watch the children from the balcony. She's going to write to Carl straight away to say she accepts.

But she promised him an answer "in two hours max" only a few minutes ago. He'll think she's mad. She has to wait. She finds some comfort in the fruity aroma of the burgundy and enjoys the light-headedness the alcohol provides.

Étienne has decided not to leave her alone. "Johar, you haven't touched your courgette flowers. Don't you like them?"

"Yes, yes, I do."

"You're not quite yourself tonight. Did you have a bad day?"

"Not at all, on the contrary, a very good day. I'm not supposed to tell you – but I can rely on your total discretion, can't I? I haven't even had time to tell you, Rémi. Carl made me a very good offer at lunchtime. I've accepted the position of CEO of Oryx."

# 11

All of a sudden, the dining room is sizzling with surprise and excitement. Étienne abruptly moves back his chair, colliding with Claudia's. All four of them stand up, hands grabbing Johar's shoulders with admiration and affection. Étienne, Rémi, and Claudia take turns to hug her. Étienne holds Johar with an insistence she finds surprising. She laughs, runs her fingers through her hair, digging them into the glossy mane, and Claudia thinks for a second that she is going to tear off her wig and throw it on the floor in a theatrical gesture. Rémi also laughs, a genuine laugh filled with wonder, like a child who has just arrived at a funfair. He puts his arm around Johar's waist and tries to draw her to him with an almost youthful clumsiness. Étienne won't stop talking, repeating Johar's name over and over, like a spell: "That's incredible, Johar, that's amazing, Johar." Then, more knowingly, "Well earned. You really earned this, Johar."

Étienne tells Claudia to get champagne. He says, with a smug little laugh, "Good thing I always keep some chilled!" and while Claudia takes out the champagne coupe, she keeps hearing him repeat, "Good thing I always have some champagne chilled," as though that's the most important detail of the evening.

Claudia returns with the coupes and lets Étienne uncork the bottle. The foam runs over outstretched hands, and raised voices drown out the clinking of the glasses. For once, Claudia has no trouble blending into the background; everybody else's cheeks are as flushed as hers, and all she has to do is laugh and keep saying, "That's amazing! Congratulations!" with the others. She even gets a kiss on the forehead from Étienne, and is surprised to be anointed by his outburst of joy in this way. Delighted, Étienne solemnly raises his glass, and everyone follows his example. "To the CEO!" he trumpets. "To the CEO!" Rémi and Claudia echo, lifting their glasses to their lips.

Claudia brings her hand down as soon as she senses the bubbles on her tongue. She must protect the unknown life developing inside her. She looks around. No one asks her why she isn't drinking or tries to guess her secret. Her gaze slides down to the courgette flowers, turned cold, untouched on Johar's plate, barely started on the others'. The beautiful, flaming orange of the corollas they had straight out of the oven has darkened, and their tips are sagging on their bellies, stuffed with whitish filling.

Suddenly a little dizzy, Claudia clutches the table. Once again, she feels a sharp pain tear through her belly, as though a scavenger is sinking its fangs into her stomach, trying to tear out a piece of flesh. The voices buzz in her ears. She hears the two men enveloping Johar with their admiration and love, and thinks about their desire to touch her, about Rémi's clumsy, animal gesture when he tried to pull her towards him. She remembers Étienne grabbing Johar by the nape of her neck and pressing her against his chest in an almost tender gesture. Claudia shivers in the evening.

Will Étienne embrace her with the same tenderness when she announces her pregnancy? The question echoes painfully and gets lost in the great void that sweeps over her from the inside. How she wishes she could be certain he would. How she wishes she could, right now, lean her head on his shoulder and feel the warmth of his large body against hers. This child rekindles the hope that throbbed in her during their first dates. This child may at last allow her to push open the door to Étienne's world, share his tastes and knowledge, and embark with him on all the journeys that were supposed to be the key to her freedom. Two years ago, Claudia clung to the promise of Étienne's love like someone adrift clings on to the hope of a lifeboat that never comes. Since then, she has let herself be sucked into the cold, grey waters of loneliness, but this child allows her once again to believe in rescue. This child stops her from drowning.

She looks up, still clutching the table. The cramp tearing at her loins has relented. Étienne is not looking at her. He doesn't see her. She is nothing. Her anxiety sinks its talons into her chest, climbs up her neck, and grabs her by the throat. What if she told him about the pregnancy straight away, to get his reassurance? She opens her mouth and closes it immediately, swallowing the mass of tears gathered in it. Of course, she can't say anything now. That would be a ridiculous way of attracting attention. She's planned to tell him over the weekend. Only three more days to sit tight with her secret. Three days before Étienne loves her again.

In an involuntary surge to muster courage, Claudia lifts her chin and clenches her fists. She hears the sound of broken glass and, without quite understanding, sees a mixture of blood and champagne in the palm of her hand, down her arm, all the way to her elbow. The delicate crystal could not withstand the pressure of her fingers. The other three are looking at her, surprised, as though irked by this ill-timed interruption.

"Oh, bother – I'm sorry, I don't know what came over me... I'm so clumsy this evening. I'm going to clean up. Don't move, Étienne, I'll do it. I'm going to rinse all this off. While I'm at it, I'll clear away, it's all gone cold, anyway. We can move on to the next course."

## 12

The words have the same effect on Johar as the sips of champagne: little waves of pleasure that start from her chest and slide down gently, spreading their warmth to her stomach. "You've earned it. You should be proud of yourself. You'll be an amazing CEO." The pleasure is more intense because it's tinted with the taboo of lying. Actually, she doesn't think she has lied to them – the word is too strong and heavy with moral judgement – only changed the order of events. She'll phone Carl in an hour, but she has taken the liberty to enjoy the outcome of this call now. Stealing one hour after waiting many years: it can't do any harm.

"Has the schedule already been fixed?"

"Carl's going to leak the news to the press tomorrow. The merger will take several months, there are unavoidable statutory and organisational steps to go through – I don't have to tell you that. I won't be officially appointed until the AGM next spring, but as soon as my name is out there,

I can start working on the project and putting my team together."

Johar enjoys the golden bubbles bursting on her tongue. She feels strong, her legs powerfully rooted in the ground, her body a focus for all the lights in the living room. If the lamps are spinning slightly around her, it's to crown her better with their shimmering rays. The excitement following her announcement has made them all warm, so they're sweating, she in particular in her thick suit trousers and long-sleeved blouse. She can feel a trickle of sweat running down her spine and wonders if darker grey rings have already formed over her buttocks. She should have worn a summer dress. Her black wrap-around would have been perfect for this moment of triumph. She pictures herself dominating the scene with her stately demeanour, her hips shown off by its elegant folds. Rémi tries to embrace her again, but she doesn't let him get hold of her; she is a statue you touch with the tips of your fingers, unsure if you're allowed to. The time when she couldn't have imagined celebrating success anywhere but in the arms of Rémi, her biggest admirer and best support, feels a long way away. Their former complicity is now totally alien to her. And yet Rémi looks genuinely happy right now, he has dropped his sour expression from earlier this evening and recovered his usual smile. Johar remembers how she used to love his constant good mood, his heavily self-deprecating sense of humour, and his almost childlike ability to marvel. She remembers how the admiration Rémi has always had for her – probably a contrast to his self-contempt – has allowed her to stay on course during the toughest times. But she no longer wants him. No longer needs him. Tonight, Johar plays the scene of her consecration alone in her head.

"Have you already picked your executive committee?"

Étienne's words reach her through what feels like a long tunnel. She focuses before replying, "You're jumping the gun! I've barely processed the news myself. Well, I guess I already know who I *don't* want in my EXCOM—"

"I'm sure you do. All the old guard who wouldn't believe in you are going to kick themselves..."

Johar senses a feverish note in Étienne's warm congratulations. She can't help deriving a perverse kind of pleasure from it. Rémi warned her yesterday that his friend was going through a hard patch professionally. She thought, *That's what happens to amateurs, they end up being exposed.* And this evening, as she studies Étienne's grey eyes and the three new lines furrowing his forehead, making him even more tragically handsome than when he was younger, she wonders if he's aware of the irony in his own words: he didn't believe in her either, no more than the old guard he is now ridiculing.

Johar met Étienne almost twenty years ago, in the flat on Rue des Saints-Pères his parents had left him after moving to Normandy. Rémi, who had arrived before her, opened the door and led her to the living room in an almost religious silence. She thought she was walking into a two-tone world, a fantastical forest where the brown of the parquet and the floor-to-ceiling bookcases mirrored the green of the velvet curtains, the antique armchairs, and the bindings of the books. She did not see Étienne at first, not until he said, "Hello, Johar," and made her jump. She looked up and saw him perched on one of the ladders to the top shelves, searching for a book he wanted to lend Rémi. He did not take the trouble to come down to welcome the newcomer. On the contrary, he used his raised vantage point to inspect her brazenly.

For years, whenever Étienne spoke to her, Johar felt that it was through the layers of culture and history that separated him from her; that it was from the height of his ladder. Only this evening, the perspective has changed. Tonight, the future CEO, the one Étienne once described as "exotic" according to Rémi's clumsy reporting, contemplates tiny Étienne from the summit of her glory.

"Excuse me?" Étienne says.

Johar said "tiny Étienne" out loud.

"Nothing, I was thinking about something else," Johar replies, labouring the last part of the sentence. She tries to say something else to change the subject, but her thoughts get lost in the fumes of alcohol cluttering her skull. She has lost the habit of drinking so much and remembers she's barely had anything to eat since this morning. She licks her parched lips. She must have a glass of water. She goes to the open window. The air is totally still, not a breath to dry her clammy skin. The two men follow her, circling like vultures. Their bodies are too close to hers and she suddenly feels as though the heat is emanating from them, their admiration a sticky mass she's struggling to escape.

She looks at Rémi's feverish smile and the beads of sweat above his upper lip, studies the smug crease in Étienne's eyes, listens to them showering her with flattery, and watches her reflection on their smooth faces until she feels nauseated, until she can no longer stand the mediocrity of this mirror. She puts down her champagne coupe, surprised to have shifted so quickly from delightful drunkenness to revulsion. Her eyes sweep the room and she glances across the living room, through the glass wall, searching for the only person who hasn't tried to smother her with flattery.

"I'm going to help Claudia in the kitchen."

Rémi and Étienne look at her, taken aback by the urgency in her voice, then decide to take it as read that two women should be left in the kitchen to prepare the meal.

# 13

"Will you keep me company on the balcony while I smoke?" Rémi asks.

"Are you trying to make me relapse?" Étienne replies absent-mindedly.

"Not at all, I'm not forcing you to smoke. But you're not going to tell me you can't stand the smell any more, are you? We can get five minutes of fresh air before the chilli in Claudia's curry hurls us into the fires of hell."

Étienne reluctantly follows Rémi. What he needs is a moment alone with Johar, not Rémi. The latter leans against the frame of the French windows, at a respectful distance from the drop. He doesn't suffer from actual vertigo, but he prefers to be cautious. He takes a half-crushed packet of cigarettes from his back pocket. His elbows on the wrought-iron railing, Étienne watches the passers-by on this ever-lengthening evening. A group of teenage girls with their arms around each other's waists walk down the boulevard, talking loudly. It's already very dark, and he gazes at the milky sheen of their round shoulders and the bare expanses of their backs that their dresses reveal.

Rémi looks with jealousy at his friend's shoulder blades protruding through his light cotton T-shirt, and at the lines on his forehead and the corners of his mouth, which make him look like a film star more than ever. Rémi thinks it's a pity Étienne no longer smokes: it would make a beautiful scene, like in a 1950s American film. He lights his cigarette, looks at the pattern formed by the plane trees, and wonders how old they are, to be tall enough to reach the fifth floor. Their leaves are turning yellow. The summer will be over soon. So much the better. Rémi is waiting impatiently for the melancholy of autumn, its gentle, subtle colours, the sound of damp leaves. He hated their Greek holidays. He feels he spent three weeks blinded by the blue glare of the sea and the whiteness of the villages, constantly assaulted by the deafening song of cicadas and the biting sun. Johar had invited two sets of their friends, couples with their children, and as soon as the pride in showing them around the huge house perched over the Mediterranean was over, Rémi realised he would have a difficult stay. Every day, he was surprised to see the others apparently loving the never-ending lunches and the afternoons when, still sticky from the salt and the sand, they would doze off under the pergola, its reeds barely shielding them from the rays of the sun. He found the monotony of days when nothing happened except swimming and eating unbearable. He had played the mine host role, since it was what everyone expected of him, but the masquerade had exhausted him.

Once the guests had left, he spent the last week doing nothing but sleeping, to recoup. This gave him a chance to spend less time alone with Johar. Their rare conversations had been laborious enough. The intrusive presence of their friends' offspring at the start of the holidays had inevitably led them to broach the subject of children. But even this topic wasn't as prickly as it used to be. When they pretended to argue about children, the ones they didn't and wouldn't ever have, it was no more than a sad act. It was a topic they now spoke of in the past tense.

At least, between Johar's endless swimming in the sea and her daily work phone calls, he'd had the chance, during their final week, to get some privacy and call Manon. The freshness in Manon's voice had the same effect on him as a sip of water on a man lost in the desert. Manon knew how to speak to him without sarcastic remarks or commands. She knew how to tell him brief anecdotes about everyday life, which moved him or made him laugh. She knew how to listen to him.

Rémi sees Étienne turn and look at him with a thoughtful expression, as though wondering whether to ask him something. Rémi hopes he's grateful to him for organising tonight's dinner. It was hard to persuade Johar. But Étienne really needed it and Rémi owes him for providing an alibi for all his little escapades with Manon.

"On second thoughts, give me a cigarette. I'm no good at playing the perfect guy. Besides, I'd better make the most of it while we still don't have kids."

"So you're really thinking about having a baby with Claudia?"

"Yeah... Apparently you have to settle down at some point, right?"

Rémi manages to feign a little laugh. The thought that Étienne could have a child and not him is actually deeply painful.

"Back in our wild youth, we never imagined this is where we'd be at forty, did we?"

Rémi wonders how to take Étienne's question. He tries to understand what exactly challenges his friend's imagination: whether it's his own rise from his upbringing among Reims shopkeepers to the peaks of the Paris business world he now frequents thanks to Johar, or Étienne's path, no doubt less dazzling than what he felt entitled to. Unless Étienne is referring to their disjointed love lives – all Rémi sees in them is profound banality.

"I don't know. I didn't imagine much in our youth, which wasn't as wild as all that, as far as I remember. I definitely didn't suspect life would be made up of so many compromises."

Étienne isn't listening to him. He takes a nervous drag on his cigarette and glances at his watch. "I have to make a call." Then, as though slightly guilty about leaving his friend so abruptly, he adds, "It won't be easy for you, becoming the boss's husband. You're taking it in your stride, with a smile. I couldn't in your shoes. Good thing you have your little Manon to take your mind off things."

Rémi shrugs. He didn't have to pretend he was excited. He has fought at Johar's side long enough, believed in her enough to be genuinely happy about her appointment. He is also somewhat relieved by it. He has supported Johar unwaveringly – even though for many years now he's known that she no longer needs him. He's been at her side until she reached her goal, despite the ravine that's grown wider between them. He went all the way. Now he is free.

## 14

Claudia hasn't heard Johar come into the kitchen. Standing on a chair, she is looking into an overhead cupboard, searching for a serving dish large enough to accommodate the mountain of curry she has prepared. She grabs a bowl speckled in green and steps back down, holding on to the cupboard with one hand.

Johar waits for her to reach the ground and for the bowl to be safely on the worktop before making her presence known.

"You're doing a balancing act. A bit careless."

Claudia is startled. She wonders for a moment if there's a hidden message in Johar's words – has she finally noticed something?

"I'm sorry, Claudia, I gave you a fright – I didn't want to bother you. Could I have a glass of water, please?"

"Yes, of course."

"Thanks."

Johar drinks the iced water in one gulp. She's drunk it too quickly, it's made her feel slightly queasy. The kitchen walls are spinning around her. The straight lines of the chequered floor have become dangerously distorted.

"Can I sit here with you for a minute?"

"Yes, of course. It's ready. The dish I'd picked was too small, and since I'm not used to these large gatherings—"

"Don't worry, take your time. Look, they're out on the balcony, talking like two old mates happy to be together again. And I feel comfortable here. It reminds me of my mother's kitchen."

Johar is surprised to hear these words escape from her. She has avoided her mother's kitchen for ten years. Each time she and Rémi reluctantly accept the invitation for lunch in Noisy-le-Sec – once a year, the maximum interval to avoid making her parents angry – she always makes sure she arrives late enough that she won't have to set foot in it.

"Really? You're lucky to have a mother who's passed on a love of cooking. Mine never had time for it. Actually, she never had time for much where her children were concerned."

*My mother didn't have time for her children either,* Johar thinks, *it was all about satisfying the monstrous hunger of the men.* As soon as this thought takes shape in her mind, deeply buried recollections resurface: recollections of holidays, dating back to a time before the sight of her mother in the kitchen began triggering her fury. She remembers her tiredness as a child, early in the morning in Tunis, body still heavy and mouth furry after the night. She would walk across the room, shutters closed, trying not to step on her cousins lying on the mattresses that took up the whole floor. She would slip into the kitchen, where her mother and her aunt would be whispering. Squatting on very low stools, the sisters would be kneading the butter-coloured semolina together. Johar would bury her tousled hair in her mother's bosom to shield her sleepy eyes from the already bright sunlight and let herself be lulled by the mysterious melody of words murmured in Arabic. When she got hungry, she would take a piece of dense and dry-crusted bread, the bread her parents would then replicate for many years in their Noisy bakery before mastering the art of the French-style baguette. She would chew her bread in silence. The hours would pass, the August stuffiness gradually invading the room, and one action followed the rest with relentless precision. The kanoun was lit on the narrow balcony, and peppers and tomatoes roasted in the embers. Her aunt would give them a regular quarter turn, always burning her fingers in the process, never even thinking of using tongs. Meanwhile, Johar's cousins would wake up and start calling her to go downstairs and play on the esplanade, but she would often choose to keep watching the show playing at eye level, the blades peeling, slicing, chopping, the hands kneading, and the tinplate saucepans rattling ever more violently on the gas cooker. She'd listen to the oil sizzling in the pans and the quiver of the couscoussier.

Johar is unable to revisit the rest through her childhood eyes. She can only think about it in the accusing light of her adult perspective. The men – her uncles, her eldest cousins, and often guests she couldn't place precisely in the family – would wait, comfortably seated at the table, for the procession of dishes. Only at the end of the meal would the women and children, sitting in a circle on low stools or crouching directly on the floor, quickly share the lukewarm leftovers. They would grab handfuls of fried food gone limp, comb through the couscous, now congealed into compact balls by the sauce, searching for a forgotten piece of meat. Then her mother would make tea. She would boil the leaves, pour out the first water – too bitter – and try it several times to make sure she had added the perfectly cloying amount of sugar the males expected. Meanwhile, her aunt would fill three large tinplate bowls with hot water and washing-up powder, and soak the dishes. The men, stuffed with fat, spice, and sugar, would go and nap while the women and older children were busy until mid-afternoon, until the time when the city, the entire country, solidified in a jelly of sleepiness and heat.

This ritual made the teenage Johar scream with rage at her mother. It was the Noisy replica, even more than the Tunisian original, that drove her crazy.

"They didn't know any different back there, so fair enough, you didn't want to upset them, but here? Don't you think he could give you a hand and invite you, his wife, to sit at the table when he has guests? Your sister doesn't work. If she fancies waking up at the crack of dawn to cook couscous for six hours, that's not my problem, but you're up early six days a week to work at the bakery, like him! So rest on the seventh!"

The first time Rémi came to her parents' for a meal, Johar threatened to leave the flat on the spot unless her mother sat down at the table with them. During the meal, which felt endless to both of them, although for different reasons, Johar stared angrily at her mother as though to nail her to the chair with her eyes and stop her from going back to the kitchen. Her mother had subsequently complied with these demands, which were always torture for her, whenever her daughter came to visit. But Johar knew that on a day-to-day basis she was still the same.

For a long time, the anger she felt at her mother's submission fuelled her rage for success. She swore to herself she would never cook. She made scrupulously sure that she and Rémi shared the daily chores with perfect equality. Above all, she decided she would become the kind of woman you couldn't picture confined to the kitchen. She would become an entirely different woman from her mother. Then one day – Johar couldn't say when exactly – her anger towards her mother dried up, and made way for arid indifference.

Johar watches Claudia's back tensing up as she lifts the heavy casserole dish and puts it on the worktop, and follows the movement of her arm as she stirs the sauce before transferring large ladlefuls of curry into the bowl; she is captivated by these actions she has sworn off since adolescence.

Claudia lifts her head to signal that everything's ready. Johar feels a little better. The floor tiles are parallel and have straight corners once again; the opaque mist around her is dispersing. Even so, she has no desire to tear herself away from the spicy warmth of the kitchen and return to the ludicrous comedy being acted out in the living room. She wants to stay cradled, for a little while longer, by the memory of the rhythmic movements and melodious voices of the women who raised her. Astounded, she realises that what she wants right now is to feel her mother stroking her temples, the pads of her fingertips always soft from being soaked in olive oil. Johar, the strong woman, Johar, the warrior, who is about to carry off a resounding victory with a phone call to her boss tonight, notices that she has a burning longing for maternal tenderness she thought she had fully extinguished. It's as though she has discovered a gaping wound, no longer sore but still there, hidden for years in the pit of her body, which only her mother's care can close. She looks at Claudia and imagines for a second that she's going to pick the most tender morsel of meat in the dish and secretly pop it into Johar's mouth, like her mother used to do.

"Can I ask you to bring the rice, Johar?"

Claudia has garnished the rice with a few pinches of saffron. In the red streak on the white dome, Johar thinks she can see a pattern like a crack.

# 15

"So, Johar, should we get our anecdotes ready for all the journalists who are going to ring us before doing a feature on you?"

"Yeah... Maybe. Readers of the so-called financial press are always more interested in that than in the company's strategy and results."

"Good thing Rémi used to tell me everything, at least before your censorship policy came into effect."

Johar smiles. She doesn't need censorship. Over time, she's managed to become a totally smooth personality with no rough patches.

Rémi swallows a mouthful of curry.

"Mmm... It's delicious, Claudia... No, I don't think I told you everything, Étienne. There was already an omertà around Johar even in the early years. Do you know, for instance, how her very first job interview at Oryx ended?"

"The one with Denis? Book Denis?"

Denis G. gave Johar a copy of *The Art of War* on the day she started her job. He kept a small stack of this ancient work in his office and took pride in turning all his young recruits into enlightened readers of the military treatise.

"Yes, well remembered, Étienne, Book Denis. The book must still be somewhere at home, nice and clean, not a single page corner turned down. You could start by telling the journalists that Johar never opened it—"

"That'd keep Denis up at night," Johar says, laughing.

"Yes, but it might do the poor guy a favour if he knew that the spotty developers he gives his book to are about as interested in it as they are in the flora of Kamchatka—"

"That's not exactly the case for me, Rémi, you have to admit. First of all, I've always had flawless skin. Secondly, it took some strategy to get there. It's just that I had no time to read…"

Back then she used to work like crazy. She'd spend her days checking lines of code, fall asleep over client presentations at night, and set her alarm to recalculate the hours on her team's invoices.

"Anyway, if I can go back to that first interview with Denis—"

"Who only agreed to see me because it never occurred to him that Johar was a woman's name—"

"Johar totally turned him around in the interview, like she does so well. She convinced him she could programme in twelve languages. She told him she'd managed all her cousins since she was four. There was no mention of 'benevolent management', luckily, so she was able to tell him she'd kept them on the straight and narrow, with the odd slap, without putting him off. Johar, the lioness, leaves the interview triumphant: the predator left her prey no escape route. As she's leaving, the guy tells her he's heading out, too, that he's going home for lunch – that's right, it was back in the days when you wouldn't get fired if you went home for a good lunch made by your wife instead of wolfing down a sandwich in twelve minutes. They exit the building together and walk down the grim road in Vitry-sur-Seine, where this obscure branch used to have its offices. And Denis sees Johar go up to an old brown Peugeot 205, where I'm waiting for her. Johar sees the guy's face cloud over, so she immediately walks away from the car. He asks her what she's doing and she replies, not skipping a beat, 'I'm keeping an eye on what this creep's doing at the wheel of his dustbin.' She then called a taxi and got it to drop her off at the nearest train station, while I sat there waiting for her like an idiot."

Étienne bursts out laughing. He remembers very clearly the awful Peugeot 205 Rémi drove when he was twenty-five. They used to joke that it was the same colour as the mud at the bottom of the Seine because that's where it had been fished out of.

"It's true, you used to drive me to all my important appointments... I felt Denis could never trust someone who travelled in that piece of scrap metal."

Rémi gathers up the precious drop of nostalgia he detects in Johar's voice. So she, too, is moved by the recollection of their early years. He has carefully stored in his memory these tales of drives that ended on the side of a country lane, waiting for a recovery vehicle with their heads resting in the weeds, of mountain hikes that ended with night falling and them running to get back because neither of them could read a map. He keeps, nice and tidy in his brain, the image of Johar in stitches whenever he came home decked out in the most extravagant wigs from the African hairdressers in Boulevard de Strasbourg, where he liked to make a small detour on his way back to Rue Cail, when he knew he would find her all in knots from the stress of her next work deadlines. He sometimes still looks through this intimate photo album with sadness. But, over the years, the snapshots have become more blurred, rarer, finally leaving the more recent pages totally blank. Johar doesn't need wigs any more. Johar isn't afraid any more. She has become a machine and mastered the art of war. Rémi wonders if she actually knows what she's fighting for.

He savours the perfectly cooked saffron rice, the sweetness of the raisins. This dish tastes like the cinnamon of his childhood winters. Rémi needs sugar now. His body craves sugar. His body craves the sugar-sweet body of Manon.

He didn't manage to see her this week, or last weekend. Rémi adds it all up. Not counting the preparation meetings with the whole teaching team for the new academic year, he has seen Manon only three times since he got back from Greece. That's not enough for him. It's no longer enough for him. He looks back on the beginning of their affair, last autumn, when he thought he was in control of this three-way game of hide-and-seek: him, Johar, and this new Physics teacher who had just joined the closed circle of the lycée's prep classes for elite university entry, so terribly attractive with her freckles and her doe eyes. Manon was intimidated by the challenge of her new job, by the pupils only just younger than herself, and by the pressure of the exam success rate; she drank in Rémi's advice greedily, and he was surprised to notice that he still had the power of seduction. She would confide in him and call him whenever she felt lost. He was surprised to see a hint of admiration in her eyes when she watched him speak in front of the other teachers. This resurgence in the attractiveness he thought had vanished had gone to his head and given him rash self-confidence. He saw the spark of desire in Manon and told himself he could play with it without getting burned. When, one afternoon when neither of them had classes, she invited him for a coffee at hers, he thought with detachment, "I'm going to cheat on Johar."

Not only did he not feel any shame towards his wife, it actually made him rather proud. Manon was single. It would be up to him to get organised, like in films; he would play the part of the married man with the double life, of the clever, calculating lover. It would be up to him to set the pace of their liaison, Manon would have to adapt – he had a wife, and not just any wife, but a powerful woman from whom it was imperative to conceal this affair. With Manon, he gladly rediscovered the intoxication of sex; he would cheerfully schedule the steamy afternoons spent in her bed, against the warmth of her body. Except that this pretend distance lasted only for a while. Rémi soon became aware that he was hungry for love. The withdrawal symptoms inflicted by Johar had been dreadful and the relapse dizzying. The whole world now looked studded with Manon's freckles; he thought of her night and day, wanted to embrace her in the middle of the staffroom. What's more, he discovered that he aroused strong feelings in Manon too. She needed to share the discovery of a new film or a piece of music with him, express to him her anger at an item in the news or her awe at the beauty of the city where she had been living only a few months. She sometimes had to suppress the desire to call him during the times of day he had forbidden, and genuinely seemed to suffer because of that. She would force him to drop the vitriolic humour which had become his way of commenting on the world. She wanted to try and understand what he thought of their mission as teachers and, more widely, their role in this society where she felt both so comfortable day-to-day and, deep down, so totally lost. She seemed to share Rémi's sorrow whenever she broached, with tact but determination, the taboo subject in his life: the absence of a child. He had not dared formulate a plan to live with her, and yet the prospect of a life without her seemed totally absurd to him now.

"Marvellous curry, Claudia," Rémi mutters, his taste buds still saturated with the softness of Manon's skin.

"Really? Thanks. I was afraid it wasn't really right for this time of year, but great if you like it. Oh shoot, I forgot the toasted almonds—"

"No big deal, Claudia," Étienne interrupts her.

"They're ready, I put them aside in a bowl, in case you didn't like them... I'll go and get them now."

Claudia feels Étienne's annoyed expression follow her. She walks across the living room, mechanically picking up Rémi's jacket, which has slid off the armchair where he'd put it. A phone slips out of the pocket and rolls onto a cushion. As Claudia kneels to put it back, a green strip flashes before her eyes.

*From: Manon*

*"You knock me sideways."*

Claudia suddenly feels Étienne's large hand give her shoulder an irked squeeze. He brings his mouth close to her ear. The restrained anger in his voice makes her shudder.

"What are you doing? Stay with us at the table, please. No one gives a damn about your almonds."

# 16

Étienne watches Claudia return to the table with the downtrodden expression of a dog that's just been thrashed by its master. He stands in the middle of the living room, tries to calm down, breathes slowly. He knows how unfair it is to offload all his violent anxiety on this poor woman, and yet he can't help seeing in Claudia's sad downturned eyes an invitation to unload the filthy rage he's drowning in. This dinner party is driving him crazy. Johar is driving him crazy. Johar, who's showing off so crassly in front of them. Johar, who's messing around with Rémi telling them youthful memories no one cares about rather than finally giving him an answer about the contract.

In the building across the boulevard, two windows that revealed cheerfully lit rooms have abruptly turned dark, two grey eyelids concealing the golden irises of that Parisian flat from him. Étienne also closes his eyes. He puts his hand on the back of the armchair where Rémi left his jacket, and tries to keep his balance.

From the pocket of his jeans, his phone emits a brief, flirtatious beep. He shouts, "I'll bring the almonds, Claudia," towards the dining room and takes refuge behind the glass wall of the kitchen to read the message he has just received. It's Alexandra, the boss of his law firm, replying to him. Having failed to grab a one-to-one conversation with Johar before dinner, and remembering that information is the key to power, Étienne decided to share the scoop about Johar's promotion with Alexandra. At 9.45 p.m. he wrote:

*"Breaking news and first-hand info – under embargo: Johar Léger will be appointed CEO of Oryx."*

It's 10.10 p.m. and Alexandra has just replied:

*"HUGE NEWS. WELL DONE."*

He lets out a moan of relief. He presses his eyeballs with his thumb and middle finger as though trying to push them together. He's not going to snivel like a kid just because Alexandra has given him a Brownie point. Behind the four words in capitals, he can hear Alexandra's exasperating nasal voice, can see the glowing white of her smile, worthy of a toothpaste commercial. She must be at home, drinking a glass of Chardonnay, seated comfortably on the terrace of her penthouse in the western *banlieue*, her toned little buttocks squeezed into the white jeans she was wearing this morning, while he, Étienne, is humiliating himself trying to charm his friend's wife. He wonders if in the privacy of her home, Alexandra's blow-dried hairstyle is still the impeccable triangle that inevitably reminds him of the Sphinx's headdress.

His phone tells him she is writing another message. His heart seems to beat in time with the tapping of Alexandra's fingers, nails varnished red. After what feels like an eternity, he is released from his wait by another life-saving beep.

*From: Alexandra*

*"Just checked in with Grégoire, who had an exchange with the W. fund this afternoon. They're not entirely sold on the prospective merger between Oryx and Neria that Carl advocates. The board of directors set the condition that Carl line up someone to succeed him. Grégoire knew they wanted a woman but didn't know who. Sounds like your Johar is Carl's only hope of being seconded by the board in his big plan."*

Étienne rereads the message several times. Alexandra may have written to him, but behind her there's Grégoire's hand, her boss, the founding father, the godfather. He looks up. Through the glass wall, beyond the living room, he sees Johar at the table, her face shining from the drink and the heat, her bosom thrust forward like a protective shield. Johar is gleaming with delight, her pride saturating the atmosphere in the room, even though she is still not aware of the full extent of her power. The thought that this woman, whom he only agreed to let into his very personal circle out of friendship for Rémi, and perhaps, at most, out of a taste for the exotic, should hold in her small, plump hands the future of a company the size of Oryx, is making him nauseous. He cannot understand why she is entitled to all this power when he has to make do with the treats Alexandra condescends to throw him. He has an exemplary professional history too. Like her, he spent sleepless nights at the office, watching out for a glow of compassion in the empty eyes of the cleaners. He thinks about his father, who pushed him to become a lawyer like himself, sniggers as he pictures the arrogant old man, always closely shaved, elegant in his anthracite suits. He understands his life now, and the disguises change nothing: his father, just like him, would prostitute himself by day to find clients, and let them rape him all night. He stupidly let himself be dragged in the old man's footsteps into the whorehouse that the business world is.

*When it comes to professional glory, I was screwed from birth in any case*, Étienne thinks in a fury. *I'm not a woman or an Arab.*

The third beep on the phone makes him jump. Alexandra, again. The letters, in a small bubble that pops up on his screen, lead a kind of malevolent round dance:

*"Since you're a close friend of Johar Léger, you must have made a deal with her that we'll be on the Oryx legal team for the merger. Grégoire and I are counting on you."*

Étienne puts the phone back in his pocket, hoping to silence it this way. He wonders where Claudia has left the stupid almonds.

He keeps telling himself that information is the key to power. For now, Johar doesn't know she is Carl's only hope to make the merger happen. In this, Étienne has an advantage over her. The question now is knowing how to use it.

## 17

Johar grabs a raisin she's left on her plate and chews its soft texture. She licks her thumb, realises she's eaten with her fingers, and laughs softly. No one seems offended. She wonders whether to eat a sprig of coriander the same way, then restrains herself. Next to her, Rémi mops up the sauce on his plate, carefully tracing an orange spiral. Incorrigibly Gallic, Johar thinks, to eat everything with bread, even a rice dish. But she's tempted to do the same, so much is she enjoying Claudia's cooking right now, so thrilled is she by the strength of the curry, the freshness of the herbs, and the sweetness of the fruit.

"Johar, do you remember the summer we planned to drive as far as Tarifa, and the car died near Vierzon?" Rémi has turned towards her, elbow on the table, holding his piece of baguette soaked in sauce, hanging on her answer. Johar is a little weary and wishes she could put an end to all these stories about their youth, but suddenly the image flashes before her, a slightly blurred snapshot drenched in light, the dream of a Spanish beach swept by the wind, and the disappointment drowned in a lukewarm beer by a motorway. She nods and lets Rémi continue. He chews his last mouthful slowly. Johar listens to him resurrect the times where they discovered they were equally insatiable for alcohol and partying, tipsy on the excitement of Johar's early successes; the drives to the country in the Peugeot 205, the nights spent drafting a future that bears no resemblance to their present day-to-day life. They were so young, still so unpolished, so touching in their hunger to live intensely that, even though she knows that words don't amount to much in comparison with years of indifference, she accepts with a mix of curiosity and gratitude this feeling of nostalgia she has pushed away with disdain all her life.

For a few more minutes, she permits herself to forget the phone call she must make to Carl, the important decision, and the glory to come.

Rémi tries to catch her eye but Johar turns her face to the window. She steeps herself in the blue-black of the sky. Here, lurking deep inside her, in the pit of her stomach, under the layers of curry, under her warrior's suit of armour, there must still be a bit of her, a part of the woman who dreamed of the freedom of an owl swaying on a branch to the whim of the wind.

Johar grabs the sprig of coriander abandoned on her plate. She munches the crenelated leaves and savours the aniseed-like taste of this last stolen moment.

# 18

The leftovers on Claudia's plate have gone cold and are starting to congeal; the small heaps of rice about to collapse under the garnish are now solid. She can only catch shreds of conversation between Johar and Rémi. She can't help staring at Rémi. Her gaze bores into the little folds at the corner of his eyes and slides down to the glistening sauce on his lips. *You knock me sideways,* she keeps repeating to herself, wishing she could feel contempt for his thick features and unattractive body. She forces herself to see Rémi as she always has: a friend of Étienne's, reassuringly bland, good-natured, warm. But now this image is superseded by that of a man capable of knocking this Manon sideways. Who can she be? She remembers the party in the Paris bar where, each in their own way, Johar and Rémi had so totally ignored her, and tries to pull the features of a woman who could be Manon from her memory. Claudia recalls a red mane flaming in the bright light of the bar, thinks she remembers a green dress swaying to the music. *This is absurd*, Claudia thinks, *why would Manon have attended that particular party, and how could I have spotted her?* Besides, she may not be a friend but rather a colleague, a neighbour, or a pupil. She is suddenly very sure of the latter, and the image of the dull teacher who has trouble dragging his students out of their boredom gives way to that of a seductive orator, popular with female pupils who crowd around him after class. Claudia would like to picture Manon as ugly and cold, only the young woman who has gatecrashed her thoughts beams with freshness and desire for Rémi. Claudia wishes she could be sure that Rémi couldn't knock anybody sideways, but she can't help feeling a pang of jealousy when she replays the brief, four-word tune she read on his phone.

Her gaze sweeps the flat looking for Étienne and stops on the figure looking lost in the depths of the kitchen. She studies the perfect angles of his profile, slightly concealed by his wild locks, and the shape of his chest. Étienne looks like a film star. He has the tragic beauty of celebrities who die too young. He's charming like the boys you fall madly in love with as a teenager, the ones you watch playing football in the school playground while you quiver with desire and frustration at the sight of a sweat-soaked shirt or a grazed knee. It's Étienne who should receive messages from all the Manons he knocks sideways, Claudia tells herself before thinking: *Perhaps he does receive them, more discreetly than Rémi.* Claudia is not jealous of these potential admirers of Étienne, of these invisible lovers. She realises with wistful resignation that Étienne's charisma no longer works on her. For the first time, surprised by her own thinking, she tells herself: *His icy perfection, his superficial charm, they're welcome to them.*

The person she envies is Manon. This Manon who is alive, throbbing, and in love. Claudia tries to persuade herself that the message she read accidentally is proof of only a banal sexual affair, a soulless fling, but the words come back to her ruthlessly. *You knock me sideways.* Claudia looks at Rémi's shoulders, always rolled forwards, and imagines them rolling over Manon as he embraces her, inhales the smell of her hair while she huddles her head against his chest, closing her eyes. Claudia thinks about this woman who can't bear the thought of Rémi spending an evening without her, who feels a compelling desire to put herself forward, even if that involves taking risks.

"Étienne, what are you doing?" Rémi shouts. "Never mind the almonds. There's nothing left of this delicious curry anyway."

Étienne returns, his face taut, silent in response to Rémi's cheerful call which is followed by another remark: "Did you get lost? Were you sending secret messages from the kitchen?"

"Not at all. I was looking for the almonds."

Then, desperately needing to offload his anger on someone, Étienne adds, "I'm not like Claudia, skulking away and snooping through your phone."

Claudia feels a wave of redness rush over her chest and spread to her face. She looks deep into her plate, wishing she could bury her face in the curry and drown in the sticky sauce. She stutters a few words and shakes her head as though to cast out of everybody's mind the absurd idea she could have done something like that. She senses a blend of confusion and pity in the looks Rémi and Johar direct at her. She's not sure what she's ashamed of more: to have got unwittingly involved in Rémi's private life, or being subjected to Étienne's aggressiveness in public.

After what feels like an interminable silence, Claudia hears Rémi stutter with a forced smile, "And there I was, thinking I could indulge all my vices in the home of my lawyer friend, protected by professional confidentiality... You're not safe anywhere."

She slowly looks up, both relieved that he has put an end to the silence about to stifle her and hurt that he chose to laugh instead of taking her side. Her gaze slides over Johar's face, lost in thought, eludes the nauseating sourness still emanating from Étienne, and pauses on Rémi. Through a fixed grin, he darts her an arrow that carries a question.

# 19

Rémi watches the patches slowly disappear from Claudia's chest. The second Étienne hinted at her alleged indiscretions with Rémi's phone, her entire neckline was steeped in red, as though her skin, paper-thin, had been dipped in a bottle of scarlet ink. The colour is now slowly fading, in blotches, forming odd geometrical shapes in the V-shaped neckline of her dress. Rémi tries to decipher in these hieroglyphics what could have embarrassed Claudia to this extent.

He's dying to go and check his phone to find out what could have alarmed her so much. But he holds back so as not to arouse Johar's suspicions. Claudia has just put a hand over her chest, as though to conceal the evidence of her crime. A little further down from her hand, under the dark fabric of her dress, Rémi makes out two stiff little mounds that make him think more of an adolescent's body than a woman's. He imagines the panic-stricken beating of her heart. What does a frightened child do when she discovers a secret that's beyond her? She keeps quiet, Rémi thinks, reassuring himself.

Unless she panics. If stupid Étienne keeps rattling her like this, Claudia could lose control, probably seek refuge in the reassuring company of a woman, and confide in Johar. Impossible, Rémi mutters to himself, impossible, Claudia can't string two sentences together. Even so, he plays the scene to himself. He pictures shouting, tears, black mascara on Claudia's pale cheeks, Johar's mouth twisted in anger, the white knuckles of her clenched fists, the words uttered in the masculine voice Johar has when in the grip of icy rage: *traitor, spineless, pathetic, coward!* The prospect makes Rémi's Adam's apple rise and fall quickly. He becomes aware that his face is taut with a fixed smile. He quickly moves on to the next scene: kicked out by his betrayed wife, the husband goes to his loving mistress. More tears, grey streaks on Manon's pretty, pink, freckly cheeks, but this time they're tears of joy. This time, the words are a balm to his bruised soul: *reunited, together, loving each other in the open.*

*Maybe I'm approaching a crossroads in my life and I can only picture it like a bad 80s series*, Rémi wonders. His self-deprecation can't conceal a more serious question: doesn't he wish this tipping point would happen today? Perhaps he has actually been waiting for chance, or fate – whatever the word used by the mediocre screenwriter of his life – to give Claudia this strange impulse to go looking through his phone in order to free him, at last, of the chains binding him to Johar? Rémi entertains this thought, examines it from different angles, like a crystal figurine he's afraid to break.

He is abruptly pulled out of his reverie by Étienne. "Johar, I imagine you've already discussed your remuneration package with Carl?"

Johar shrugs, but Étienne isn't discouraged. He starts listing and comparing the salaries of all the large company directors he knows.

*It's not like him to talk about money so bluntly*, Rémi thinks, *it's too crass*. In Étienne's world, one usually doesn't mention money, even if it's everywhere, even if it's concealed under the perfect hang of a shirt, the feline silhouette of a car, the velvety elegance of a wine. Moreover, it was Étienne who trained Rémi in the art of suggesting rather than saying, where money is concerned. Back then, Rémi was an ordinary spectator, not having the means to play. He often wondered why Étienne didn't confine their friendship to their university desks and Quartier Latin cafés, why he opened the doors to private sports clubs and exclusive parties to him. Then Rémi realised that, in order to enjoy luxury fully, you need an audience. The free-flowing champagne found no better mirror than Rémi's innocent eyes, the madness of an improvised jaunt to Marrakech found no better echo than in his credulous ears.

Later, thanks to Johar's spectacular ascent, Rémi was able to enter that world in turn. The Michelin-starred restaurants and remote destinations stopped being chimeras.

He could tread the narrow, cobbled streets of Capri with the ease of someone who felt at home, and go into a connoisseur's raptures over the perfect preparation of a meat reduction at the table of a renowned chef. He learned the art of choosing gifts that reflect who you are rather than aim to please the receiver, serving fresh truffles to friends after a weekend in the Périgord and promising to restock others soon with black pepper just brought back from Cambodia. When visiting Paris, his astounded parents were able to enjoy the comfort of a guest room in the spacious flat their son and his wife had moved into.

Rémi considers that there will be no more of this if he breaks up with Johar. A feeling of rebellion sweeps over him at the thought of being thrown out of this garden of the wealthy. While Étienne keeps stunning Johar with astronomical figures, Rémi throws himself into a mental calculation exercise: he adds his salary to Manon's, deducts the cost of Paris rent, and is depressed by the slim result. *Two ordinary teachers*, Rémi thinks, *we'd have the lifestyle of two ordinary teachers.*

Manon lives on the sixth floor of a building with no lift in the Quartier Latin. Since Rémi has known her, he's loved slipping through the claws of the waiters who relentlessly collar the tourists, and into a stairwell that's too dark, climbing four steps at a time, and sitting on the rickety sofa that stands on the crooked parquet. He feels young, he feels free, like a character in a novel. Around the bed where they make love in the middle of the afternoon, stacks of books on the floor form the ramparts of a fortress. And yet as he pictures his own library coming to join Manon's paper Lego bricks, his stuff cluttering her pretty attic nest, Rémi wonders if he would still appreciate the freshness of Manon's nook. He is not sure he could give up comfort for the love of her.

Rémi also wonders, sheepishly, if Manon would still be as happy to see him if he was no longer able to dazzle her with a flower bouquet too large to fit in her doorway, if he could no longer make her dream by telling her about all the cities he has visited and promising to take her there. Étienne often teases him by asking him what a woman like Manon could possibly see in him. He has persuaded himself that their relationship rests on the solid foundations of shared tastes and desires. But tonight he's not sure he wants to put his theory to the test.

# 20

Johar stands up, goes to pick up an empty plate to take to the kitchen, but then yields to the lure of the balcony that overlooks the languid city. "I'm going for a smoke," she says.

"I'll keep you company," Étienne immediately responds.

She suppresses a sigh.

As soon as Johar steps through the French windows, she is struck by how gentle the evening air is now. The stifling late-August heat has relented. She rests her elbows on the railing and lets her head drop forward. Her hair stays in its stiff, full block, refusing to follow the movement of her head. She pats the base of her mane to expose her sweaty nape. Her gaze sweeps over the black mass of the tall plane trees and their foliage that throbs in time with the twitching in the air. She imagines her head dragging her forward all the way, pictures herself tipping into the void, nosediving before spreading her wings and letting herself be carried by the rising currents.

"I've been waiting for a moment alone with you."

Étienne has uttered these words in a solemn tone, enunciating every syllable. Johar's reverie hits the ground. She looks up at him.

"I have access to some information that's very important for you. About Carl and the merger. I don't think he's told you everything."

He pauses theatrically.

"I'm going out on a limb telling you this, but I'm doing it for you. And I know you'll remember it when the time comes."

Johar listens as Étienne reveals to her the sine qua non condition for the merger between Oryx and Neria, Carl's dream. He explains to her, his eyes feverish with excitement, that she has a formidable asset in her hands, a card just waiting to be turned into gold.

"I don't know what you've told Carl, and I don't want to meddle in your financial negotiations, but you should toy with him for a little while. Let him believe you're hesitating, so he offers you all he can. I know it's not your style, that you're straightforward and loyal, but there are opportunities in life that just shouldn't be missed."

Then he places his hand on Johar's, still clutching the wrought-iron railing, warm from having stored up the sun's rays all day. "And you wouldn't be stealing anything from anyone by doing that. They say women have trouble measuring their worth in the workplace. You will truly have deserved this. You can't expect less than all the bosses I mentioned earlier. You don't realise it. You tick all the boxes."

Johar closes her eyes, as though this could silence Étienne. Of course, that's how he sees her: she ticks all the boxes. Female. Young. Visibly from a minority background – especially when, like tonight, her hairstyling lets her down. A software engineer. Risen through the ranks. Étienne doesn't mention her talent, her drive, or her vision for the future. He takes comfort from seeing in her success only what separates her from him.

She opens her eyes again, extricates herself from Étienne's hold, and waves away imaginary midges flying in front of her. Étienne has finished his monologue and is staring at her intently, waiting for her reaction. *He's just put me in a cage,* Johar thinks, *and he wants me to be grateful to him.* So, the board of directors has already chosen her to be the boss. Others have already decided for her without her knowledge. She no longer belongs to herself. She is a marionette whose strings are being pulled by men in suits. She thinks about Carl, about his brilliant acting talent, about his ability to appear detached when inside he must have been chomping at the bit during their lunch. She pictures him seething with anger right now, behind the gleaming screen of his phone. She really must call him now.

She is surprised by Étienne's feverishness, by how fast his attractive poise and composure have given way to panic-stricken eagerness. It almost makes her feel sorry for him. Étienne makes her think of the childhood places you revisit as an adult: he has shrunk. Later, she'll see what crumbs she can give him.

Now, all she wants is to finally smoke her cigarette in peace. Even those on death row are entitled to one last cigarette.

"All right, Étienne. Thanks for the information. Very useful. I need to be alone for a moment, so I can think this over – you don't mind, do you?"

## 21

Claudia considers her reflection in the steel lid for a moment, before stepping on the pedal abruptly. When the bin opens its gaping mouth, a sickly-sweet smell escapes from its plastic belly. Among the damp cartons and peelings, Claudia sees the purple surface of the chicken giblets. *I should have taken the rubbish down before dinner,* she tells herself, suppressing a retch. She scrapes the plates carefully with a spoon and watches the small clumps of sauce-soaked rice fall with a dull thud on the carpet of detritus. She opens the dishwasher. A cloying smell makes her throat feel constricted and she immediately closes it. Rémi has come in, carrying the dishes. In the white and green bowl, the curry sauce, now dark orange, forms a gelatinous pool with a few chunks of meat and vegetables floating in it.

"Put everything on the table, Rémi. I'll sort it out later."

"Don't you want me at least to put the leftovers in the fridge? You've got enough for a romantic feast tomorrow."

"Thanks, that's very kind. I'll take care of it."

Rémi doesn't seem to want to budge. She tries to fight off the wave of heat that attacks her neckline once again and forget about the pain gnawing at her belly.

"We had a nice time," Rémi says gently. "Quite apart from the fact that your cooking is exceptional, I mean." He pauses. "And completely apart from the happy news."

Claudia is startled by his words before she realises that Rémi is referring to Johar's promotion. She is surprised by his choice of words, by his transposing the expressions usually used for describing life's landmark events to Johar's career.

"I'm glad you've enjoyed the evening," Claudia replies flatly.

But Rémi will not be discouraged and tries to find another foothold.

"You and Étienne still look so young and in love."

Claudia feels her mouth twitch slightly and wonders if Rémi is really daring to make fun of her so brazenly.

"You don't know about the compromises you need to keep going long-term. You haven't turned into acrobats yet, constantly walking the relationship tightrope which threatens to tip into friendship, indifference, or hate at any minute. Tonight you've given us a little prod to get us to straighten up."

Then, searching for a spark of sympathy in Claudia's eyes, Rémi concludes in a whisper, "It's infinitely precious."

Fine, she gets it. Rémi has nothing to fear. She won't mention Manon's message, won't say anything to Johar, or

Étienne, or anybody. Now can he leave her alone and let her take a breath before the final hurdle of dessert?

Claudia nods, trying to make Rémi understand that he can go back to the living room with peace of mind. Then she freezes. She has seen a glistening wet patch on the black tile on which she is standing. Her eyes grow still, staring at the floor. A small puddle has formed between her feet. Claudia grips the table. Her heart beats furiously against the walls of her chest. She feels a wetness between her thighs and down her calves. She stops breathing. She tries to stamp a smile on her face in the hope that Rémi won't see the angst that is battering her, and that he won't follow the direction of her gaze, uncontrollably drawn to the floor. The puddle spreads with unbearable slowness. Claudia is glued to the lazy progress of the liquid escaping from her body. She sees it reach beyond the edge of the black tile, over the cement seal, and finally, on the immaculate whiteness of the white tile, reveal the depth of its blood-red colour.

## 22

Rémi is about to serve ladlefuls of mouth-watering chocolate mousse onto plates decorated with tropical flowers. Johar grabs her phone from the table.

"The lady of the house has asked me to wait on you," Rémi announces, interpreting Johar's silence as a mark of surprise.

"Well done. How lovely to see a man at work." Then, after a brief hesitation, she adds, "I'll be back in five minutes."

"You're fleeing temptation," Rémi replies with a smile.

"Yes, that must be it. Start without me. Isn't Claudia here?" she asks, puzzled, looking in the direction of the kitchen.

"She's coming," Rémi says.

Johar reaches the hallway before heading down the corridor with the bedrooms. She thinks she recalls Étienne turning one of them into an office. She can call Carl in peace from there.

She stops outside the closed door, glances around to make sure Claudia isn't nearby, and smells her armpits. Their pungent odour makes her grimace. She takes two more steps and slips through the half-open door to the bathroom. The floor and walls are clad in terrazzo tiles. Johar smiles at finding the coating, speckled in multicoloured fragments, that she remembers in the modest hallway of her aunt's building in Tunis here in this bourgeois flat. In front of her, two round basins seem to balance on a plank of natural wood. She wonders if Étienne has refurbished the bathroom recently, or if he already had two sinks when he was living alone, brushing his teeth over one or the other, depending on his mood. She approaches one of them and opens the tap, cupping her hands under the icy trickle and plunging her face into them. For a few seconds, she enjoys the sting of the cold water on her cheeks. She resists the urge to run her wet hands through her hair, for fear of making its kink worse. There is a carefully arranged stack of beige towels on the wooden stand next to her. Johar takes one and rubs her forehead and cheeks with it. In the mirror opposite her, her face looks weary. Her cheekbones, once high and proud, have receded. The arcs that connected the base of her nose and the corners of her mouth now stretch down towards her chin. She forces a smile to rekindle the comforting image of the gap between her front teeth, but gives up immediately in order to stop seeing the little wrinkles that form instantly at the corners of her eyes. *You're getting old, darling*, she tells herself. She unbuttons the top of her blouse, washes her hands with soap, and rinses her armpits, which she then dabs with the towel. *I'll be totally ready for my talk with Carl*, she says to convince herself, although she knows she is only stalling.

As soon as she closes the mixer tap, Johar hears a dull, intense sound, like a wheeze. She rushes out of the bathroom. The sound seems to be coming from the nearby toilet. She tries to open the door but finds it locked. The sound has stopped. Johar waits outside the door. The wheezing resumes, hoarse and stifled, with intermittent, sharper moans. *It's Claudia*, she thinks.

Johar immediately catches herself thinking, *I haven't got time to waste on her, I barely know her, I have to call Carl.* She heads towards the office, then stops, her fingers on the door handle. *Look at the machine you've turned into. Look at the monster of indifference they've made of you.*

She turns back and gently taps on the toilet door. "Claudia? Claudia, is something wrong?" The wheezing falls silent. Johar presses her breast and her ear to the door and, to her surprise, repeats the words she has heard her mother whisper to her a thousand times: "I'm here if you need me." There is another wheeze, then a voice responds, hesitant and frail, like a thread Johar decides not to let go of.

"Johar?"

"Yes, it's me. Tell me what I can do for you."

"Can I ask you – can you go into my bedroom – you know which one it is? Can you open the wardrobe and bring me a pair of pants and a dress – any you find."

The voice dies down, as though swallowed by pain. Johar thinks she can hear another moan, fainter this time. After a few moments of silence, Claudia adds, "And my phone, please. It's on the chest of drawers."

"Yes, of course."

"Thank you so much."

Johar hesitates, then asks very softly, "Do you want me to get Étienne?"

Another silence. "No. Don't say anything to him. Please."

## 23

Claudia has fallen silent. She places a hand on her belly. The spasms that tormented her a few minutes ago have subsided as abruptly as they started. The bleeding has stopped. She slips her pants, stained in black liquid, down her legs and throws them into the bin, over the paper towels with which she wiped the kitchen floor. She holds on to the small sink to stand back up. She wets a few sheets of toilet paper and wipes away the blood that is beginning to dry between her thighs and calves.

She closes her eyes. She doesn't want to know and yet she has to know. She slowly turns around. In the white enamelled bowl, she sees fragments of flesh, shreds of life, floating in a red pool. Even though she is struggling to stay standing, she refuses to sit back down over this scarlet wreckage. She leans back against the wall, listening out for Johar's footsteps in the corridor. She can't wait for Johar to return and, at the same time, dreads the loneliness that will follow. She feels like a child waiting for her mother's kiss, with a mixture of yearning and fear, aware that it will be the last for that evening. The sight of blood everywhere distresses her. She can't bring herself to flush the toilet. She puts the lid down and shuts the bin. Silence gradually fills the room, chilling her ankles, knees, and hips. But Johar is back, her voice warm and gentle, an unexpected solace.

"Claudia, I've found everything. Will you open the door or would you rather I left your things outside?"

"You can leave them outside, thanks." Then, immediately scared that her curt reply may dismiss the woman who has come to her aid, she adds, "Johar, could you possibly come back in ten minutes?"

"Yes, of course."

The footsteps move away. Claudia opens the door gently, picks up the small parcel on the floor, and locks herself back in. She strips. In the bathroom mirror, her body looks healthy and alive, with no visible marks of her bruising. She examines the shape of her belly, still slightly domed. She doesn't know what to do with her stained dress. She doesn't feel like rinsing it in the handbasin, seeing the blood splashing over the walls and eddying down the drain. She rolls it up into a ball and stuffs it into the bin. She puts on the pants and navy-blue dress Johar has picked for her. She could leave the toilet and slip into her bedroom, which is very close, without too much chance of being discovered. But she's scared, so dreadfully scared, scared of the shadows haunting the long corridor, scared that her own death is lurking behind the door, scared of abandoning the wreckage of herself under the plastic lid of the toilet.

She unlocks her phone and scrolls down her list of contacts. It's impossible to speak to her mother. She could call her eldest sister, Paola, the only one of her siblings she is truly close to, but she didn't tell her about her pregnancy – she's afraid Paola will be cross with her, and she's too tired to find the right words to justify her secrecy. The same applies to the few female friends she could turn to. A name she hasn't thought of appears on the list. As she left her last appointment with the gynaecologist, she stored the number Audrey Edelman had scribbled on a card. "You can call me. If you ever need to, or just if you feel like it," she had said in her calm, trust-inspiring way. This evening, Claudia internally replies that she needs her, that she needs her more than ever, while wondering if she dares disturb someone who is actually almost a stranger at nightfall in August. Then she thinks of Johar, of her unexpected gentleness towards her, and suddenly wants to believe in the motherly benevolence of all women.

"Doctor Edelman?"

The gynaecologist sounds neither surprised nor annoyed by her call. Claudia talks and the doctor asks questions, using plain words interspersed with a few silences interrupted only by her usual deep humming.

"You must come to the hospital so I can examine you, Claudia. I'm on duty in the maternity ward. I don't think you live far from here, do you? I can't give you a prognosis on your pregnancy without having more information."

But Claudia knows more for herself. The stories her mother would tell about the joys and sorrows of her patients have given her enough insight on the subject. She gives a detailed description of the violent cramps, then the blood, the torrent of blood, and, finally, the solid fragments torn painfully from her body. She leads the doctor to utter, very gently, what she was afraid to say to herself.

"It sounds like you've had a miscarriage, Claudia. I'm so sorry."

At these words, Claudia feels as dazed as when, as a child, she pestered her parents until they admitted that the childhood myths – Santa Claus, the tooth fairy, and the Easter bunny, all of them – were the fruits of adult imagination. She knew but didn't want to know. She would have preferred them to keep up the pretence a little longer.

The gynaecologist adds, "In any case, you must come to the hospital tonight. It's not very urgent, since you've stopped bleeding, so get some rest and change your clothes, but you must come. Can your husband bring you?"

Claudia says nothing. As she escaped from the kitchen, praying that no one would see her, she glimpsed Étienne's angular shape in the living room. It seemed impossible to reconcile the intimate tragedy taking place inside her with the utterly alien body language of this man. Audrey Edelman's question seems even more incongruous than if she were suggesting that Johar bring her.

"No, I don't think so."

"All right. Can you take a taxi?"

"Yes."

"Good. I'll be here all night. You must go to the maternity ward emergency department."

Claudia feels a vague sense of distress rise inside her, a black, unfamiliar angst. As though she has guessed, Doctor Edelman says, very gently, "It's natural to be upset. Unfortunately, it sounds like I can no longer take care of your baby, but I will take care of you, Claudia."

# 24

Johar sits in the armchair facing Étienne's light wood desk. She pulls on the thin brass chain of the lamp in front of her. The opaline glass shade gives a green light that illuminates the folders stacked on the desk, and the bookshelves cladding the walls. She drums her fingertips on the leather blotter. Claudia's moans still echo in her ears.

Johar puts her phone on the desk. She can't bring herself to call Carl straight away. She decides to ring her mother. She has delayed this moment all day to avoid the neverending recriminations – "you don't come and see us often enough", "you're ashamed of us", and, of course, "you didn't give us grandchildren".

"Johar?"

Her mother's cry is like that of a drowning woman. She has breathed in her daughter's name the way she would gasp for one last breath of air. Although she has never heard it until now, Johar instantly recognises the tone, which, all over the world, heralds bad news.

"Johar! Dad died."

For a few seconds that feel like an eternity, Johar is overwhelmed by a question to which she dreads the answer: *Whose dad, Maman – my dad or your dad?* She keeps silent, suspended from this tenuous moment.

As though the solemnity of this announcement required it to be uttered in all languages, her mother repeats, this time in Arabic, "Abi maat."

*Abi*, Johar thinks, *she said "my" father*. She suppresses a dreadful laugh. Her own father, Johar's, isn't dead, she can see him again, even tonight if she feels like it, kiss his strong cheeks and gently blow on the flour on his apron, she can talk to him about anything and everything, and even ask him to forgive her for the lost time.

"Johar…"

Her mother has a head voice, a youthful voice at odds with her now grey locks. But tonight her voice is no longer that of a young woman, it has gone back to that of a little girl. "I thought I wouldn't be able to reach you. I thought you'd never want to answer me again."

Johar feels a painful mass obstruct her throat, a large lump of tears she presses on to prevent it from bursting. She feels guilty for worsening the distress of the woman who has always promised to be there for her if anything is wrong. Her reply takes shape slowly and she hears her own words, both so banal and so genuinely yearning to dress her mother's wound. "I'm sorry, Maman. I'm sorry for your loss. I wish you could have been by his side. I wish I could have seen him one more time too."

Johar estimates her grandfather's age. She realises it's been almost twenty years since she last saw him, because she never had the time or the inclination. The image she keeps of this erect, skinny man whose language she didn't speak doesn't tally with the very old man he became. She would occasionally ask her mother after him, she knew he was slowly being killed by cancer, but the distance and the years had made her grandfather an abstraction. Oddly, his death seems to restore his flesh to him. His death rekindles in Johar the memory of his hand patting her forehead when she would fall asleep among the adults sitting and chatting outdoors in the evening, in Tunis, a hand as rough as the woollen rug on which she would be lying.

"He'll be buried the day after tomorrow. You know how quickly our people do things. With all this heat." The sentence trails off in a murmur. "Could you come?"

For a moment, Johar leaves the little girl with the salt-and-pepper hair who is whispering on the phone, she leaves the old man in his eternal, baggy sarouel trousers to return to Carl. Carl is probably waiting for her call with the same feverishness as her mother was just a few minutes ago. Carl can't wait to receive the assurance that his soldier will follow the path he has traced and that by doing so she will make it possible for him to carry on playing the great game of chess he has devoted his life to. In between flashes of anger, he must be wondering what kind of quirk is preventing the woman who has always dreamed of this offer from leaping at it. *Good question*, Johar thinks, and, for the first time, she forms a dizzyingly clear answer: *Because I don't want it any more.*

And, in her mother's pleading, Johar suddenly hears the quiver of a promise. This request, bathed in motherly love, brings her what it has always brought her: total confidence in what she is.

"Of course. I'll go to the funeral with you, Maman."

Then, slowly, with the solemnity of a woman who knows that the words she is uttering have the magical ability to transform reality, she adds, "I'll stay there a few weeks. As a matter of fact, I'd decided to take a break from my job. I want to spend some time with you in Tunisia, if you're all right with that."

## 25

Claudia looks in the toilet mirror at the image of the young woman with pale features, and calmly states to her, "It's over." The face in front of her remains impassive, the eyes stay dry. The words echo for a moment, then die out, meaningless. "It's over," Claudia says again, thinking about the hope she nurtured that her pregnancy would give her relationship with Étienne a second wind, about her dream of a brand new life that would brighten the colours of their prematurely faded relationship. No doubt Étienne would have been happy to hear she was pregnant; he genuinely seems to want a child. Perhaps he would even have viewed her differently as a mother, taken an interest in the family they were beginning to create. Perhaps. Claudia tells herself that she has lost the chance to be loved by Étienne again, or to be loved by Étienne at all, but her eyes are stubbornly dry.

"It's over," she repeats, and this time she remembers how she imagined acquiring a new status through maternity, a clearly defined place in this world. Now, she is nothing specific, she is part of a sisterhood with too many members: a physiotherapist who didn't even try to be a doctor; the understated partner chosen by Étienne to take care of their day-to-day life. She is the woman people ask questions without really listening to the answers, the woman Rémi talks to only out of politeness or vested interest, the woman who freezes with fear at the very mention of the responsibilities that fall to Johar. Soon, she could have been a mother. One of those women whose role in this world cannot be questioned, since they are here to protect and raise their children. She will not – not straight away – be a part of this caste. For a while longer, she will have to simply be herself, be content with the uncomfortable limits of her being, face the exhausting absurdity of her existence. This prospect doesn't really make her feel sad either. It is as though she had already resigned herself to it a long time ago.

These miserable thoughts spin around her. She hates herself for being so unbearably self-centred and feels like wounding herself, hurting herself, hurting herself more and more. She spits in her own face: "Maybe, deep down, you wanted to lose this baby."

This baby. The word came from Doctor Edelman. "I can't take care of your baby any more," she said, and Claudia is surprised to have made this word her own. She realises that for some weeks now she has thought a lot about herself, but never really about this other life that was beginning to develop inside her.

"Your baby." Strangely, the picture forming before her eyes is not that of a newborn, nor even of an infant, but of a little girl of three or four. It comes from a scene she witnessed several years ago, during a summer spent with Paola. She and her sister had travelled through a few sleepy Mediterranean islands, changing from ferries to mopeds, swept by the wind of euphoria that blows you along when you're no longer a teenager but not quite an adult yet. The end of the summer holidays was nearing. That day, Claudia was reading on the beach, at the time of day when the sun's attacks turn into caresses. The evening hues coated everything around her with their poetry. She struggled to focus on her book, the title of which is the only missing detail from an otherwise very precise tableau etched in her memory. She was enjoying the warm sand running between her toes, watching the increasingly few tourists on the beach, and getting drunk on the lapping of the sea. Next to her, a little girl, her skin browned by the sun, was crouching in the sand, playing. All of a sudden, as though brutally overcome by a huge wave of tiredness, the child stood up and went to lie on the stomach of her mother, who was keeping an eye on her from a deckchair a few metres away. The little girl fell asleep instantly, her face, concealed in the jumble of dark curls, buried in the dip of her mother's chest, her dangling limbs stretched like the tentacles of the octopuses the island's fishermen would dry in the sun. She was breathing deeply, almost snoring, and Claudia pictured her lips, half-open as she breathed, squashed against her mother's breast. The contrast between the vigour of this small body, active only a few seconds earlier, and the child's total abandon as soon as she was in contact with her mother's skin, was striking. Her proudly arched back and the insolent stiffness of her domed chest, a silent declaration of independence, had given way to a succession of soft curves. While the mother mechanically stroked the little girl's back, downy like a chick, while she gently ran her fingers through her curls, tousled by salt and sweat, Claudia was impregnated with the feeling of softness and absolute trust that emerged from this tableau.

*My baby*, Claudia thinks, and it seems like this soft body clinging to hers has been torn from her, that a huge gulf has appeared in the pit of her belly. *My baby*, she repeats, and a sob that felt stifled in her for years clears a way through the depth of her throat, and the sobs are now gushing out in all their fury, and she bites her hand to try and conceal their roar. Of course she didn't want to lose her child, she had already prepared a loving cocoon to welcome it, and the gap left behind fills her with grief.

And yet she notices that there's not just sadness in her tears but a desire, a fierce longing. The whole of Claudia is quivering with a longing for love, so much so that she wishes she could scream this longing for love. She wants to love as a mother and as a woman. She wants to be knocked sideways like Manon in her man's arms, she wants to hold the salty, warm body of her child against her, like the woman on the beach.

# 26

"I get the feeling our women have run away from us..." Rémi mutters.

"Yeah. I don't know what they're up to. Start if you like. Claudia's desserts are always a great success."

Rémi greedily swallows several spoonfuls. The mousse is sweet and soft. His lips, brown with chocolate, stretch into a contented smile.

"You're right to build up your strength," Étienne says. "You're going to need it."

"What do you mean?"

"I'm thinking about Johar's new position again. It won't be easy – either for her or for you."

"I stopped worrying about Johar's work a long time ago. She's in her element in the company now. She knows everything and everyone there by heart. I'm really quite surprised that all the wheeler-dealing there still gets her excited. I get the impression she's always playing the same game—"

"You don't get it, do you? We're talking about heading up a listed company here."

Rémi doesn't reply, so taken aback is he by the contempt in his friend's voice. Only a few minutes ago, making the most of their partners' absence, the two men were happily delving into memories of their student days. His old partner in crime has just stepped aside and given way to the arrogant lawyer lecturing the mere teacher.

"On the contrary, I think I understand very well," Rémi says with a huff. "Johar often tells me how it works in there, you know. You'd be disappointed. It's the same pettiness as everywhere, the same so-called strategies that are only in place to flatter egos. Johar's strength is that she can play this game to perfection, without ever forgetting that it's an act."

"Yes, but it won't just be an internal act any more. As far as clients are concerned, and especially the market, the buck stops with her now."

"She's used to it. She's been on the board for ages. And she understands completely that nobody is really judged on their performance—"

"But it's something else to become number one. She'll be envied and attacked from all sides. She'll be on constant display. You won't see each other any more, Rémi, she'll have no more time for you. She'll be totally alone, and you won't be able to be there for her."

Rémi wonders what Étienne is driving at. He feels that it's pointless to argue. He'd like to return to the previous topic, to rekindle the memory of the electric atmosphere of the bars in Rue de la Huchette, where the two law graduates would hang out and flirt with women. He'd like to revive the greedy delight with which they checked out the toned calves of high-school girls. But it's too late.

Étienne hasn't touched his dessert. He nervously beats time on the table with the handle of his spoon. Rémi looks at his friend's clamped jaw and the hard lines of his mouth. Johar doesn't need to wait to be formally appointed to arouse resentment and jealousy. Still, he wonders what it is that's annoying Étienne so much this evening. Johar's promotion should be good news for him, it should ease the negotiations that this whole dinner party has been an excuse for. Étienne mentioned some difficulties at work, the growing pressure he was under from the partners at his law firm, as though he was genuinely afraid things could take a bad turn. Rémi knows that Étienne is in no danger. He walks in the footsteps of a father who knows the whole Parisian scene. Even supposing some temporary weakness were to push him off the red carpet of his current firm, he would immediately find a job somewhere else, just because of his surname. Besides, Étienne doesn't need money: he could live off the rent from the properties bestowed on him by his parents. He must be imagining problems out of boredom, to break the monotony of a life where everything is written in advance. Rémi would like to ask him why he has wiped out the one touch of creativity he allowed himself in this ocean of conformity, why he gave up on his bachelor life to move in with this young woman who appears to bore him to death.

But this thought brings up the painful memory of Étienne's plans for fatherhood, so Rémi keeps quiet.

He feels contaminated by his friend's sourness, and experiences a dark pleasure picturing him getting old. He imagines the alluring lines of his angular face hardening with the years, his cheeks growing hollow, his small, sharp eyes becoming lost in their protruding sockets. He thinks of the young, charming, sparkling intellectual who'd taken him in the moment he had smiled, twenty years earlier, and tells himself that Étienne will end up sad and frustrated because he decided to pour himself into a mould that's too tight for him.

Rémi takes another spoonful of chocolate mousse, and the sugar sweetens his mood. He looks at Étienne with a little more pity, a little less anger. If Étienne's arrogance didn't make him deaf to all comments, Rémi would advise him to forget his obsession with appearances for a moment, to stop tormenting himself over the ups and downs of a career he'll soon forget about, to escape from this prison he's shut himself in with Claudia. He remembers thinking earlier that Étienne had put Claudia in a cage, but he was wrong. These two are together behind the same bars. He thinks how lucky he is to have met Manon. Coming into contact with her, he had felt totally sucked in by another human being again, swallowed up by the desire to know all the nooks of her body and mind. He wishes he could take refuge in the warmth of Manon's arms right now and be rocked by the music of her words.

"I'm going to make a phone call," he announces to Étienne, since apparently it's the moment of truce for everyone.

"Who are you calling?"

Rémi glances towards the living room. "Manon."

"Your young teacher? Now? Must be serious."

Rémi doesn't know if he's meant to hear a note of sarcasm or a spark of envy in his friend's words.

"Seems to be. Increasingly so."

"You start enjoying the young ones just as I start drifting away from them."

Rémi wants to point out that Manon is only slightly younger than Claudia, but Étienne continues, "It's too dangerous. We think having them by our side makes us younger, until one day we realise they've made us into old fools."

"Don't you think it's your sudden urge to settle down that makes you an old fool?"

"Stop it. You want me to carry on seeing twenty-year-olds? Now? The world's on its head."

"I didn't mean twenty-year-olds," Rémi says, but Étienne isn't listening to him.

"I must say, it's tempting. There's a new intern at the firm, you should see her. She tries to dress all grown-up, but still oozes adolescence through every pore. She only ever wears grey, but when you get close to her, you feel like you're diving into candyfloss, rosy skin everywhere. I think her name's Léa…"

Rémi stands up and walks out backwards, letting Étienne lose himself in the soft memory of Léa.

# 27

Johar gently shuts the office door behind her. She approaches the toilet, but hears no sound. She lightly taps three times. No response.

"Claudia?" she murmurs.

She slowly pushes down on the handle. The light is off, the toilet empty. She thinks she hears movement from the bedroom and walks down the corridor. The parquet creaks under her feet. Without thinking, she removes her stilettos and carries on barefoot. She sees a photograph in front of her that she didn't notice earlier. It's a view from a window, with the frame in the shot. For a moment, in the corridor's semi-darkness, Johar was taken in and thought it really was an opening onto the street. She stops. The window overlooks what appears to be an abandoned garden. She remembers the desire she had, earlier, to fly off Étienne's balcony. Then she thinks about calling her mother and about the decision she has just made, which still feels surreal.

Through the half-open bedroom door, Johar sees Claudia putting things into her handbag. She taps again to signal her presence. She sees a glimmer of fear in Claudia's face, but it vanishes as soon as their eyes meet. Johar walks into the room and sits down on the bed. She feels the soft woollen rug under her bare feet.

"Thanks for coming, Johar."

"Of course. What are you doing?"

Johar doesn't need to say what happened to Claudia out loud. The secret they share now transcends words, held in all the new intimacy with which two women talk to each other.

"I've got to go to hospital."

Johar hears a veil of sadness in Claudia's voice, and also a new note, a strength she has not detected until now.

"Is Étienne going with you?" Johar asks, even though she already knows the answer.

"No."

"Then I'll come with you."

"No, there's no need. I'm going to take a taxi."

"I'd better come with you, Claudia."

"No, really. I'm sure. Certain. I'm better. It's not that..."

"Then what is it? Please tell me how I can help you." Johar smiles at Claudia gently. "I don't know what you want to do, Claudia, but you'll manage it. Just tell me how I can help you."

"I'd like you to create a diversion. So that I can leave discreetly. So they don't see me."

"All right." Johar gets up. "Can you give me five minutes? I'll make one last phone call, then I'll help you disappear."

"Fine, go ahead. I have to finish getting my things ready anyway."

"I'll come and get you."

Johar is back in Étienne's office in a few steps. She wonders if, just as she saw a new strength dawn in Claudia, Claudia noticed a new strength take hold of her, Johar. She anchors her feet to the floor, sits back firmly against the back of the leather armchair, and takes out her phone.

# 28

Rémi picks up his jacket from the back of one of the living room armchairs, puts it on, and immediately feels the comforting weight of the phone in his pocket.

He takes a stride over the step and is out on the balcony. His chest tightens at the sight of the fifteen metres that separate him from the ground. Without Étienne at his side, his vertigo is more pronounced. He feels as though he is seeing himself from the window opposite, a man foolishly standing on a narrow stone ledge over the abyss. The arabesque patterns in the wrought-iron railing want to lure him into their mesmerising dance, draw him into the void. The pots of lavender at his feet threaten to trip him up. Rémi presses his shoulder against the reassuring surface of the door frame and grips the metal of a folded-back shutter. He stares resolutely straight ahead.

He's going to have to overcome his vertigo, because there is nowhere else he can comfortably call Manon. *Your guests are running away from you, dear Étienne,* Rémi says mentally. The thought of Johar and Claudia both disappearing down the corridors worms itself into his mind. *They must be talking, and what can they be talking about except him and Manon?* He dismisses this thought, which instantly gives way to Étienne's remark about "the young ones". So that's how he sees his relationship with Manon. But perhaps that's how it should be seen, the banal story of a forty-something whose fear of ageing pushes him into the arms of a young woman.

There is, of course, something that overwhelms him in Manon's youth, in the fresh roundness of her cheeks, in the innocence with which she sees the world. He recalls a stroll they took together on the banks of the Seine at the beginning of the summer. The quays that day were heaving with young people eager to enjoy the first rays of sun. Manon looked out of place in that crowd of sophisticated Parisians with her little leather bag worn too long, her faded jeans cut too simply. Rémi rediscovered the beauty of the city through her enthusiastic eyes. "I love the way Parisians think their city belongs only to them," Manon said. "I mean, the way every Parisian thinks the city belongs only to him or her. They brag about Paris being cosmopolitan, but every waiter smoking his cigarette outside his café seems to want you to feel that you're treading on his patch." She tripped on a flagstone and held on to him, bursting out laughing. He prolonged that moment, taking advantage of the sweet contact with her skin, the warmth of her body, with its slightly too evident curves that she, on the other hand, didn't seem the least embarrassed about.

Manon likes who she is. She feels like an outsider, but has no need for camouflage. She knows she is imperfect, but owns every square centimetre of her body. He remembers the young Rémi fresh from his provincial hometown, in a rush to master the codes of the Parisian middle class as quickly as possible, eager to erase all the little social quirks that could possibly make his new friends snigger.

A dog's high-pitched bark makes him look down into the street. The road rushes up to his eyes and revolves around his face. He clutches the phone in his pocket. In that pocket, there's a message from Manon. In that pocket, Manon is coming to his rescue. Obviously he can't let Claudia decide how his relationship will continue. Or Johar, for that matter. Rémi still has a lot of affection and friendship for Johar, fears his infidelity will hurt her, but he knows perfectly well that the sterile cohabitation they've now had for many months, many years, is sad both for her and for him.

When Rémi takes the phone out of his pocket, he feels his blood throb violently in his neck. His gaze slowly drops from the mesh of the plane trees to the luminous screen.

Manon has written, *"You knock me sideways."*

*Good*, Rémi thinks. *Then let's fall down together.*

A ringtone, and, immediately afterwards, Manon's voice.

"You wouldn't reply. Are you angry? I'm sorry, Rémi, I don't know what came over me, you told me not to text you, especially when you're with your wife, but you see, I'm bursting at times, I don't understand what's holding you back, we could—"

"Slow down, Manon, wait—"

"You say I must wait, but I just can't understand what we're waiting for."

"I want to be with you, too. To be with you for good. I'm going to tell Johar tonight."

# 29

"Good evening, Johar."

Carl's voice is alluring, authoritative.

Johar starts slowly. "Carl, I'm calling a bit late, I'm sorry."

"No problem. As you can imagine, these days I'm up to my eyes in Oryx, no matter what time of day or night. Have you had a chance to think about it like you wanted?"

"Yes."

"And talk it over with your husband?"

"Yes." Then, after a brief pause, Johar says, "Carl, you won't be happy with my answer, but I've thought it through very carefully. And definitively."

The silence on the other end of the line becomes cold, metallic.

"I am not accepting the post, Carl. I don't feel like it. I've lost the spark. It would be a bad idea, for the company as well as for me."

"You've lost the spark?"

His voice, like ice, slithers behind Johar's ear and slides down her neck.

"No. I have other plans."

"Johar, what are you playing at? Have you had another offer – is that what you're trying to tell me?"

"No, I don't mean professional plans."

"What do you mean?" Carl pauses for a few seconds, then says, "Remind me, how old are you?"

*Too old to have a child*, Johar replies in her head, trying to forget Carl's rudeness by pretending she did not understand.

"Listen, Carl. Oryx has allowed me access to a wide range of jobs and exceptional levels of responsibility. I think I can also say, without blowing my own trumpet, that I've contributed significantly to the growth and transformation of the company. But now—"

"I don't need to listen to your platitudes. I expect more of you than that. Are you really refusing this position? Because if this is a game for getting your hands on something else, it's too subtle for me."

"I really am refusing the position."

"Do you understand the consequences of this decision?" Carl seems to be choking with anger, then continues, "Obviously not. You're telling me you love the company, but do you realise the harm you're doing it? And the harm you're doing me?"

*He's trying to appeal to my pity after humiliating me*, Johar thinks. *A bit presumptuous to make fun of my so-called games when his own are so clumsy.*

"You know perfectly well that I'm not indispensable to Oryx. It was one of the first things you taught me: no one is indispensable in a company. You and I spent years proving it."

"I don't know what's going through your mind, but I'd like to remind you that, whatever your plans may be, I can make them fail. If you've absorbed lesson number one, then you probably remember number two: I'm not a man you refuse anything whatsoever to…"

And now a threat. Johar closes her eyes, as though the darkness could stifle Carl's remarks. But his words keep drumming in her ear. Carl is spitting out his anger. Carl is screaming his panic. Then, after a little while, as though saturated with his own violence, he calms down.

"You're not going to change your mind, then?"

"No."

"Very well. Pascal will take care of the procedure for you leaving."

"All right."

"It goes without saying that neither this conversation nor my offer ever existed, is that clear?"

"Yes. You needn't worry about that."

Carl hangs up. She gets lost in her thoughts for a moment, remembering the words she expected to hear: words of comfort and gratitude, words that would have etched all they had achieved together in their memories. She's still naïve, after all that.

Stunned by the brutality of the conversation, Johar slowly lets it go, feels her blood flow back down her arm, watches the colour return to her knuckles. She's taken a few blows, but the life pulsating in her is still here, fully present.

# 30

The corridor is now totally dark. Johar feels her way down the few metres to the bedroom.

"Claudia? I've finished. I'm all yours."

She gets the impression she has snatched Claudia from a deep trance. Claudia picks up the large overnight bag at her feet and loops the strap over her shoulder.

"Do you still want me to divert attention while you leave?"

Claudia quietly nods.

"Fine. I'll go back there first and make sure they follow me into the kitchen. I'll make an announcement that will knock the breath out of them for a little while. How does that sound?"

They walk down the corridor without a word. In a few minutes, Claudia will disappear behind the heavy reinforced door, and no doubt from Johar's life at the same time. Johar wishes she could tell her what a decisive role she has just unwittingly played in her life. She wishes she could also encourage Claudia along her own path, whatever it may be. She simply gives her arm a gentle squeeze.

Johar walks, determined and at peace. Cloaked in the protective shadow of the corridor, Claudia looks at the motionless living room and rests her gaze on Étienne's broad back as he sits alone at the table. She thinks, *Tonight I decided to stop enduring this existence of mine. Tonight I promised to take life on.*

"Johar," she calls softly.

Johar turns around, surprised. "Yes?"

"I'm going to talk to him. Can you please sit in the living room?"

Hearing them, Étienne turns to them and stares at her, puzzled. Claudia heads to the front door, holds the handle lightly, and waits for Étienne to catch up with her. As he approaches, a grimace of annoyance twists his attractive mouth and he brushes away a rebellious lock of hair, revealing his increasingly knitted eyebrows. Claudia clings to the fierce yearning for love that took possession of her a little earlier. She straightens and thinks about the little life that left her before she had the chance to enjoy its arrival. *That life belongs to my history alone,* Claudia thinks, *it's still written in my body and will always be there, in a way.* She decides not to say anything to Étienne about the baby.

"What's come over you, Claudia? Where do you think you're going?" Étienne says, stepping in between the front door and her.

*I've never left anyone,* Claudia thinks, *I don't know the words.* She looks towards the living room and sees the reassuring tilt of Johar's head.

"I'm leaving," she starts to say.

"You're leaving?" Étienne hisses at her, his face pushed against hers. "What are you on about, in the middle of dinner, where are you going?"

"I'm going for good."

Étienne clenches his jaw.

"I don't see how we could be happy together, Étienne. There is no affection or desire between us. Tonight I realised that our relationship didn't make sense any more, or made no sense full stop, and I think you've known that for a long time."

"And you couldn't find a more ridiculous time to tell me that?"

"I'm sorry. Something happened... I need to leave now and I had to tell you. Forget the circumstances for a second and think about us, Étienne. One of us had to have the courage to end this pathetic little farce."

"Claudia, stop your tantrum this minute. Please. Whatever's happened to you and whatever it is you have to say to me can wait till we're alone."

Étienne tries to restrain his voice, but bursts of rage cut through its deaf refrain. He looks at Claudia, at her slender neck within reach of his large hand; his gaze sweeps over her face searching for a sign of nervousness, a quiver in her mouth. His rising anger collides with Claudia's surprising confidence.

Disconcerted, he sees again the blend of resolution and gentleness that fascinated him when she was his physiotherapist. He listens to her explain that she can decide what is good for her and for him. He wishes he could crush Claudia, push her to the floor and kick her, again and again, to punish her for what she is inflicting on him.

But Claudia continues, "No, Étienne, it can't wait. Listen to me. You don't know me, and you haven't tried to get to know me. I mistook your need to seduce me for love, but that flame has gone out completely. You don't open up to me, you don't give me anything of yourself. Maybe what you're looking for is a female companion, but what I want is desire and tenderness. I want intimacy and shared dreams. I want love."

Claudia has raised her voice. Johar turns to look at them. Claudia clings to her gaze.

Étienne can feel Johar's eyes boring into his shoulder blades. He wonders if she senses the wave of fury spreading down his spine. He tries to control his shaking hand as it pushes down on the door handle. The brass feels strangely warm in contact with his frozen fingers. He briefly hesitates and takes a step back. Claudia seizes the opportunity to slip out of the flat.

## 31

Rémi is snatched from the tenderness of Manon's voice by the slamming front door.

"I've got to go. I'll call you back."

The violent beating of Rémi's heart makes him sway and threatens to lure him into the void again. His panic-stricken brain tries to understand the meaning of the sound he has just heard. He thinks something dramatic must have happened, that Claudia must have told Johar everything and that Johar must have walked out of the flat with a clatter. Holding on to the window frame, he steps down from the balcony. The dining room, deserted and majestically illuminated, makes him think of a theatre stage before the actors come on. In contrast, the living room, timidly lit by a small globe on a coffee table, is plunged into shadow. There, Rémi sees Johar, sitting on the sofa, silent and calm, eyes fixed on the front door. He can't restrain a sigh of relief.

He approaches her, but before he's had the chance to ask her what happened, Étienne joins them in the living room. His face, which has a grey tone from the faint light, is like a commedia dell'arte mask.

"Claudia wasn't feeling well tonight," he says in a voice that's too high-pitched. "She's sorry she couldn't say goodbye before she left." Then he adds, "Sit down, Rémi."

Rémi takes a seat next to Johar, in the audience row. Étienne sits in the armchair opposite them. Under the papier mâché mask, his pupils, dilated in the semi-darkness of the room, have a spark of insanity. Rémi looks down to avoid their icy glare. He catches sight of a chocolate stain on his lower belly, where small love handles keep pulling on his shirt button. He starts scratching the brown circle with his fingernail.

Johar is holding her knee in her interlaced fingers and gently rocking back and forth. She furtively catches Rémi's eye. "Perhaps we should go..." she starts to say, but is interrupted by Étienne's automaton-like voice.

"Would you like a coffee, a decaf?"

"No thanks, Étienne."

"You can't leave yet. We've barely had time to talk about your appointment, Johar. You said you needed time to think about the confidential information I shared with you. I think you should do it, as soon as possible. You must strike while the iron is hot. We can draw up a negotiation strategy together, now, so you can call Carl tonight."

Rémi looks at his wife's impassive face, then at Étienne's tense body. He wonders what they mean.

"I've just spoken to Carl," Johar says nonchalantly.

Étienne's expression freezes. The three pronounced lines across his forehead furrow it deeper than usual.

"He doesn't want me for the position any more. He's changed his plans." Then she says, very slowly, "I will never be the CEO of Oryx."

Rémi detects no note of disappointment in her voice. He tries to come up with some words of comfort, but can't find any. He dismisses the insidious thought that this turnaround could endanger the promise he made Manon.

Étienne bursts out into a strangled laugh. "That's impossible. Carl can't do that. Offer you a job and go back on his word. That would be unprofessional to an unheard-of degree."

Johar just shrugs.

"That's impossible," Étienne repeats. "Alexandra told me barely an hour ago that you were the cornerstone of this merger. It won't happen without you."

"I've just had a long conversation with him," Johar replies. "There's no shadow of a doubt." Then, not giving Étienne time to refute the evidence again, she adds, "We're off now, Étienne. I'm tired."

Rémi stands up. He gives the table one last glance, looks with sadness at the heap of chocolate mousse whose creamy sides have barely been dented by the guests. He joins Johar in the hallway and gently squeezes her arm. She smiles at this comforting gesture, the same she used with Claudia a little earlier. *We've become each other's clones, Rémi and I,* she thinks. *Fifteen years of living together has made us invent our own sign language.*

Rémi's hand lingers on her, searching in the reassuring contact with this body he knows by heart for an answer to the questions wracking his mind, an indication as to which direction to take.

Étienne has followed them without a word. Just as Johar opens the door, he yelps, "One final question: do you know if the merger will happen anyway?"

"I don't know," Johar murmurs. "Perhaps. Probably. Carl is someone who doesn't give up. He'll get what he wants."

The couple sneak out through the half-open door. The light comes on in the stairwell. Rémi looks, relieved, at the shimmering red carpet that runs all the way down the wooden stairs. He does not turn to see the curtain fall on the wretched king who hosted them this evening.

## 32

Étienne sits down, knees apart, his long arms spreadeagled on the back of the sofa. He wonders where Claudia might have gone so late. She always gave him the impression she didn't have any strong friendships. A pretty girl tossed about by life, whom he could anchor to him firmly. Maybe she'll be back in a few minutes' or a few hours' time, choking with remorse, begging him to take her back. He wishes she would do that, for the pleasure of sending her away or, even better, leaving her sobbing outside the door, firmly shut, until an irritated neighbour asks her to go and blubber somewhere else. He mentally revisits his first encounter with that painfully shy physiotherapist, and remembers how he wanted to possess the cool hands that relaxed the tightness in his back. He obsessed about Claudia for a surprisingly long time, in comparison with his average conquest, because her pathological shyness made her harder to seduce. Then he thought she would be the ideal candidate as a companion to his life as a settled man: she seemed unaware of her allure, her self-esteem was too low for her to feel anything but gratitude towards him, she was too reserved to risk depriving him of his freedom. He wonders what mysterious path has led this timid bird to demand her right to love so fiercely tonight.

He thinks about Rémi's words earlier, about the pleasure his friend took in throwing in his face that his, Étienne's, plan to start a family made him into an old fool. Rémi was probably jealous, Étienne tells himself. He seized the chance to vent his frustration at the wreck his marriage to Johar has become. His outburst was totally unfounded. Anyway, so what if Rémi is right? It's not up to Claudia to decide what's right for Étienne and what isn't. He has always been and will always be the master of his decisions. Claudia didn't understand a thing. She's welcome to go back to her mediocre life, to the monotonous parade of her miserable patients, to the sad, lonely routine she had before living with him. She can rent another rabbit hutch of an attic, where she'll go and urinate between the cupboard and the kitchen. She could have lived comfortably with him, discovered countries where her uncouth parents have never taken her, she could have learned from his experience and his knowledge. She could have become an interesting, educated, wealthy woman. He wants to call Claudia and scream his rage at her. He didn't have a chance to do it earlier because he was too worried Johar would realise what was happening. He stupidly kept quiet in order to spare the woman who would, a few minutes later, turn out to be totally useless to his business. The only thought that brings him relief right now is imagining Johar's disappointment. He saw very well that she wasn't telling him everything, that she was trying to protect herself. But, Étienne persuades himself, the truth is irrevocable: she, who pictured herself at the highest peak, she, who inflicted her intolerable arrogance on him all evening, who tried to play with him like a cat with a mouse, has ended up alone in her fall.

Étienne gets up, walks around the armchairs, takes out his phone and frantically puts it back again. He resists the temptation to call Claudia – that would be giving her too much importance. He could ring Alexandra, but what's the use of bringing her into this train wreck? He briefly considers contacting Léa, the attractive intern. He must have her number in an email somewhere, but the prospect of experiencing another rejection is more than he could bear.

Tonight, Étienne feels abandoned. He sits on the rug, hugging his knees, his head drooping forward pathetically. Through the window, he makes out the sad outline of the plane trees that line the boulevard, their tops perfectly trimmed. *How my horizon has shrunk*, Étienne thinks. *I'm like a rat going round and round in its cage, a cage that's only slightly bigger than Claudia's, but, in the final analysis, what's the difference? Without protesting, I swallow the dreams they stuff me with, dreams of a family, a career, possessions.* Étienne lets himself roll to the side and ends up spread on the floor, staring at the moulding on the ceiling. A desire to weep rises from deep in his throat, a damp anger that only wants to explode.

He presses two fingers against his eyeballs and breathes slowly. He will not cry. He will not feel sorry for himself. He will not give in to the childish nostalgia of his lost desires. He sits up and forces himself to scrutinise the walls around him, the centenarian wisdom of his flat, the furniture and items selected with a defined taste, the books as so many witness statements that he belongs to the history and culture of the ruling class.

*Claudia is replaceable and will be replaced,* Étienne decides, *and I'll go and get that contract from Carl if I have to tear it off him with my teeth.*

Étienne does not belong to the category of people who give in to regrets. He is from the caste of those the world owes a living.

# 33

Johar looks at the orange halos of the lamp posts on the pavement. She walks slowly, watching her shadow stretch and disappear entirely before taking shape again in the next circle. Her footsteps echo on the asphalt. Paris seems to have finally dozed off. Ahead, a narrow street runs off the boulevard and forks towards central Paris. The building caught in the vice of the two roads ends in a sharp angle, at the top of which proudly stand two balconies, like a ship with a female figurehead on the bow. Johar allows her eyes to wander up the façade, up to the starless sky.

She senses Rémi at her side.

"Johar, where are you going? Don't you want me to call a taxi?"

"I'd quite like for us to walk home."

"Walk? It'll take us two hours!"

"We can start at least. We're not in a rush."

"Johar..."

She stops and Rémi looks at her with a worried expression.

"How are you feeling?" he asks.

"I don't know."

Rémi stands opposite her. The dark gives his normally cheerful face a sombre expression. His stubble emphasises the severe tightness of his jaw. His eyes, with their grey rings and bushy eyebrows, squint as though he's trying to work out what is hidden behind his wife's impassive mask. Johar owes him an explanation. But so many things happened for her tonight that she doesn't know where to begin. She takes Rémi by the arm and resumes her walk. She needs a few minutes to find the right words. She notices that Rémi hangs heavily on her arm, as though embarrassed by her silence.

"Johar, I have something to tell you."

Johar slows down. She is surprised that he is not waiting for her to speak but needs her to listen to him instead.

"The timing is probably terrible, Johar. But I don't feel I can lie to you any longer."

Johar pauses slightly. And yet she knows, she guessed that there was a lover a long time ago, but she'd always thought it was a diversion, no more than a fling. She had always believed that the end of her relationship with Rémi would be written by two hands, not three. She feels a twinge of disappointment, a pang of anger. She tries to be reasonable. After all, Rémi also has the right to choose his path.

"You want to tell me about the other woman, don't you?" she murmurs.

Rémi looks at her, speechless.

"Keep walking, Rémi. Remember, we have a two-hour journey."

She stares ahead now, and senses that he is doing the same. Walking helps them: their eyes focus on the crossings and the junctions, their voices follow parallel paths instead of confronting each other.

"Yes. You know, I never thought I'd cheat on you one day. I've always thought it was too cowardly, too banal for us. But it happened... It started because I needed reassurance, maybe also with a tiny desire to get my own back – not on you, but on this life where I feel I don't amount to much... and, quite simply, I've fallen in love."

"In love?"

"Yes. I wasn't expecting it. She is so much younger and so different from me—"

"Rémi, I don't think I want to know any more about her."

"I'm sorry."

"It upsets me, but I understand. I understand you want to be in love again. I understand that you can't be content with our friendship any more."

"I felt like I was drying up, Johar."

"I know. Me too." Johar is surprised to hear her voice break with emotion. It is not sadness she feels, but deep nostalgia.

"If you guessed, how come you never said anything?" Rémi says.

"I don't know. I was waiting. I think I was unconsciously waiting to understand what it meant for me, I wanted to know where I was heading."

"And?"

"I also have something to tell you, Rémi. It's not Carl who changed his mind about the position. It's me who didn't want it. I want to have a break. I need to understand some things about myself and my family. I know it sounds trite, but I feel I've lost sight of who I am."

Rémi says nothing for a moment.

"What will you do?"

"I'm going to Tunisia tomorrow. I'm going to my grandfather's funeral. I'll stay there as long as I need to."

Johar feels Rémi clasp her arm tighter. An ambulance siren tears through the stillness of the night. Johar looks up at the phantasmagorical outlines of the trees in the night. She thinks she can make out movement in the branches and imagines for a second that she is being watched by the yellow eyes of an owl. The ambulance has quieted down. Johar savours the city's restored calm. She realises that Rémi has, no doubt without meaning to, fallen in step with her. Two shadows glide in unison on the asphalt of Boulevard Raspail, two silences that echo each other.

# 34

"Do you mind the radio, madame?"

The taxi driver's voice snatches Claudia from her thoughts.

"No, it's fine, thank you."

She hasn't paid attention to the music until now. She listens. Through the loudspeakers, the melancholy voice of Otis Redding celebrates the ships rolling into the bay. Claudia wishes she could, like the singer, waste time, lose herself watching the tide wash over the sleeping city, be lulled by the jolts of the car taking her to the hospital. She thinks she could close her eyes, doze off, and the driver, afraid to wake her, would drive through the streets of Paris without stopping.

She opens the window and leans her head out until a breeze caresses her face. She looks up at the hideous black silhouette of Montparnasse Tower. *We're almost there. Just a few more minutes and the taxi will drop me off outside the hospital gate.* She imagines her imminent encounter with Doctor Edelman and clings to the promise of her deep, comforting voice. She will soon have to put on a hospital gown, fuzzy from having been washed a thousand times, lie down on an examining table covered with a paper sheet, and abandon her body to the doctor's exploration and treatment. She wonders if she'll need an anaesthetic to remove the last debris of the nest she meticulously prepared in the pit of her belly. The thought of losing consciousness, of disappearing into the fog of artificial sleep, reassures her agitated mind. She feels exhausted, worn out by her talk with Étienne, unable to think about the stages to come. She wishes she could forget that, however long she stays in hospital – a few minutes, a few hours, overnight at most – she will afterwards have to find a flat, wake up every morning, go to work, lay the foundations of a new life.

The taxi stops at a traffic light. Claudia remembers the almost animal instinct with which Johar came to her aid, the trust with which she let Johar take care of her. She admires the ability human lives have to resonate with each other at times. She takes a deep breath and exhales slowly.

"Is everything all right, madame?" the driver asks.

"Yes," Claudia replies. "Everything will be all right."

She could stay with Paola for a while. She knows her sister will come and pick her up from the hospital, no matter what time she calls her, and that she'll offer her the comfort of her little Italian coffee pot and the warmth of her kitchen, and that she'll surround her with love. *And then, and then, what will become of you?* an inner voice asks insistently. *And then,* Claudia replies, *I'll take my time. I'll accept this unexpected sadness, I'll observe the strange void left in my body by this life I never realised took up so much space. And I'll cultivate this new strength, this fierce desire to live and love.*

"Here we are, madame," the driver says.

The austere mass of the hospital rises firmly before her. Claudia stands on the pavement for a few seconds, motionless. A little later, day will break. Claudia is ready.

Foundry Editions
40 Randolph Street
London NW1 0SR
United Kingdom

First published as *Un simple dîner* by Cécile Tlili, © Calmann-Lévy, 2023

Translation © Katherine Gregor 2025

This first edition published by Foundry Editions in 2025

The moral right of Cécile Tlili to be identified as the Author of this work has been asserted in accordance with the Copyright, Designs and Patents Act 1988.

A CIP record for this title is available from the British Library.

ISBN 978-1-0686934-2-7

Series cover design by Murmurs Design
Designed and typeset in LfA Aluminia by Tetragon, London
Printed and bound in Great Britain by TJ Books, Padstow

All rights reserved. No part of this publication may be reproduced, stored in a retrieval system, or transmitted in any form or by any means, electronic, mechanical, photocopying, recording, or otherwise, without prior permission in writing from Foundry Editions.

foundryeditions.co.uk

This book is supported by the Institut français (Royaume-Uni) as part of the Burgess programme.

EU GPSR authorised representative: Logos Europe, 9 rue Nicolas Poussin, 17000 La Rochelle, France; contact@logoseurope.eu.

KARIM KATTAN
*The Palace on the Higher Hill*
Translation by Jeffrey Zuckerman
PALESTINE

Faysal, a young Palestinian man in exile, gets a mysterious letter about the death of an aunt he can't remember. He leaves his life in Europe behind and returns to Palestine, to the village of his birth and his extraordinary, deserted family house, the Palace on the Higher Hill. As he roams its once glorious rooms and the threat of occupation gets ever nearer, voices from the past return to shed light on his own family's story and on the story of his people.

Through its beautifully written story and unforgettable cast of characters, who occupy a dizzying space between the imaginary and the real, *The Palace on the Higher Hill* gives a nuanced, human, and deeply moving panorama of the tragedy of conflict and brings English-speaking readers an unexpected, furious vision of Palestine that feels entirely new.

*The Palace on the Higher Hill* won the 2021 Prix des Cinq Continents de la Francophonie.

## CHIARA VALERIO
## *The Little I Knew*
Translation by Ailsa Wood

ITALY

In Scauri, an end of the line seaside town forty miles or so from Rome, Vittoria dies unexpectedly in her bath. Whilst the townsfolk meet the event with sad but respectful southern Italian silence, Lea, the town lawyer, wants to investigate. Who was Vittoria, what were her secrets, why had she mysteriously arrived in Scauri thirty years earlier? And was her relationship with Lea all that it seemed?

Novelist, editor, critic, cultural commentator and mathematician Chiara Valerio is a sensation in Italy and *The Little I Knew* is a huge bestseller. It was shortlisted for the 2024 Premio Strega.

> "Enigmatic and beguiling, precise and unsettling, this seductive novel opens with a mysterious death, asking compelling questions about desire, knowability and the still limited possibilities of freedom for women. Chiara Valerio is a major talent, and she makes the small town of Scauri, between Rome and Naples, a place of fascination."
>
> OLIVIA LAING

> "With wit, subtlety and charm, Valerio captures the complex currents of secrecy and desire that is just under the surface of small-town and family life. A beguiling, atmospheric story of female fascinations."
>
> SARAH WATERS

## ANNA PAZOS
### *Killing the Nerve*
Translation by Laura McGloughlin and Charlotte Coombe
SPAIN/CATALONIA

In this tour de force of auto-journalism, brilliant young Catalan writer Anna Pazos explores the end of youth and the beginning of adulthood for the global nomad generation. Part memoir, part travelogue, *Killing the Nerve* describes Anna's odyssey to escape the "mediocrity" of bourgeois Barcelona life.

With unflinching candour and writing that is as cool as it is razor-sharp, she turns her sardonic journalist's eye on her unstructured Erasmus days in Thessaloniki, her first posting with a newspaper in Jerusalem, her sail across the Atlantic with an unsuitable lover, and her stint in post-#MeToo, pre-pandemic New York. Returning to Barcelona in 2021, when the pandemic takes hold, she then turns her attention to her own family's story, to Catalan society since the referendum of 2017, and after all her travels, she explores what it means to come home.

This stunning debut was longlisted for the Premi Finestres 2023 and voted best Catalan Book of the Year by *El País*.

**FOUNDRY EDITIONS**

1 CONSTANTIA SOTERIOU (CYPRUS)
*Brandy Sour*
tr. from Greek by Lina Protopapa

2 MARIA GRAZIA CALANDRONE (ITALY)
*Your Little Matter*
tr. from Italian by Antonella Lettieri

3 ROSA RIBAS (SPAIN)
*Far*
tr. from Spanish by Charlotte Coombe

4 ABDELAZIZ BARAKA SAKIN (SUDAN)
*Samahani*
tr. from Arabic by Mayada Ibrahim and Adil Babikir

5 ESTHER GARCÍA LLOVET (SPAIN)
*Spanish Beauty*
tr. from Spanish by Richard Village

6 KARIM KATTAN (PALESTINE)
*The Palace on the Higher Hill*
tr. from French by Jeffrey Zuckerman

7 CÉCILE TLILI (FRANCE)
*Just a Little Dinner*
tr. from French by Katherine Gregor

8 CHIARA VALERIO (ITALY)
*The Little I Knew*
tr. from Italian by Ailsa Wood

9 ANNA PAZOS (SPAIN/CATALONIA)
*Killing the Nerve*
tr. from Catalan by Charlotte Coombe and Laura McGloughlin

10 MATTEO MELCHIORRE (ITALY)
*The Duke*
tr. from Italian by Antonella Lettieri